When Ryan ... her hand and picked her u... ..., Kelly squealed, "What are you doing?"

"Sweeping you off your feet—what do you think?" he said dryly.

Kelly flushed at his sarcasm. "Please put me down," she said, an odd, husky quality in her voice.

Plainly it was a surrender, and she watched for the look of triumph to appear on his face. It didn't. "Is something wrong?" she asked nervously when he finally put her down.

"It's difficult," he said mockingly, "to treat you like my little sister. I have no brotherly feelings toward you."

"No, you've made your dislike of me quite plain."

"Dislike?" He laughed incredulously. "I wish what I felt for you were that simple."

Scottish born **ALISON FRASER** presently lives in Hertfordshire, England, with her husband and three dogs. After specializing in English and Social Sciences at Aberdeen University, she taught mathematics at London and Birmingham schools for five years, then was a computer programmer for five years for a Midlands engineering firm. Her first book, written as relaxation from work, was not publishable, but she persisted. Though she says writing doesn't come easily, she enjoys the idea of people gaining pleasure from her books. Reading, bridge and backgammon are among her other interests.

Books by Alison Fraser

HARLEQUIN PRESENTS
697—PRINCESS
721—THE PRICE OF FREEDOM
745—COMING HOME
865—A MAN WORTH KNOWING

ALISON FRASER

a lifetime and beyond

Harlequin Books

TORONTO • NEW YORK • LONDON
AMSTERDAM • PARIS • SYDNEY • HAMBURG
STOCKHOLM • ATHENS • TOKYO • MILAN

Harlequin Presents first edition January 1989
ISBN 0-373-11135-5

Original hardcover edition published in 1988
by Mills & Boon Limited

CHAPTER ONE

'YOU actually *expected* the Best Actress to go to Rhea?' Lauren James echoed, raising finely pencilled eyebrows in surprise.

And Stella Martin smiled with all the superiority of the longer-established film star. 'Of course...didn't you?'

'Well, I suppose *Sunset Gold* was the best thing she ever did,' Lauren conceded grudgingly.

'Perhaps—but it's certainly not the reason she got the award.'

'Then why?'

'I'd have thought *that* was obvious,' Stella claimed, again with a superior air.

Lauren's lips twisted slightly before she shrugged. 'Well, she could hardly have slept with all the judges...*this* year, at any rate.'

The slanderous comment drew a husky laugh, proving that nothing was sacred in their circle—least of all the fact that Rhea Cormack had died a bare four months earlier in a car crash.

'Exactly the reason she won,' Stella declared. 'I mean, you know how sentimental the business is. Why, even I shed a tear or two, and I couldn't stand her.'

'Beat you to a part, did she?' Lauren suggested slyly.

'Don't be bitchy, darling,' Stella reproved in her languid drawl, then, draining her Martini, glanced around for a waiter.

One appeared almost instantly, emerging from behind a screen of potted plants at the far corner of the conservatory. The Hotel Arbois was renowned for its efficient but unobtrusive service and, although some distance from Cannes, was a favourite haunt of the film set.

Stella Martin gave her order simply by waving a hand towards the empty glass and, when the waiter retreated, continued as if there had been no interruption, 'After all, I'd scarcely be going after the same roles as a woman of forty.'

'She wasn't *forty*,' Lauren exclaimed.

'If a day... Not on her press hand-outs, of course, but her daughter Kelly must be in her late teens by now. Speaking of which——' Stella broke off to survey the stretch of private beach beneath them '—that's her down there, standing along from the steps.'

Curious, Lauren craned her long, elegant neck to peer out of the nearest window. 'The blonde in the blue bikini? I thought that was Dale Bryant's daughter.'

'It is,' Stella confirmed. 'Believe it or not, Rhea's off-spring is the girl beside her—the short one with the dark, messy hair.'

For a moment, the two women studied Kelly Cormack, unaware that their interest was shared by the man seated at a table behind them. Unaware, in fact, that he'd been listening to their conversation from the second they'd mentioned Rhea Cormack's name.

Now he followed the direction of their gaze to the daughter, and his first reaction was surprise. She was certainly small in stature, a bare few inches over five feet, with a figure that seemed almost childishly slight in a white swimsuit. Her hair was a wild riot of black curls and, with her strong, cleft chin, generous mouth and high, slanting cheekbones, she was altogether quite different from the other girls on the beach. Yet no one could ever call her plain.

'She's not a bit like Rhea, is she?' Lauren finally remarked. 'Who was her father, anyway?'

'That's open to debate,' Stella shrugged. 'Odds on favourite was some French film director. Rhea never confirmed it, though. In fact, she generally kept very quiet about the daughter's existence.'

'It's certainly news to me,' Lauren admitted. 'I've been around Hollywood a few years now, and I don't recall ever seeing that girl before.'

'*You* probably wouldn't have.' Stella's voice held a touch of condescension. 'She was packed off some-where when she was about fourteen...for one reason or another.'

Lauren caught her meaning and drawled, 'Yes, teenagers can be rather ageing. Especially if you're trying to stay thirty.'

Both women laughed, oblivious to the effect their malicious humour had on the man. With their backs to him, neither could see Ryan Devlin clenching his glass in anger, finding nothing amusing about the way Rhea Cormack had treated her daughter.

He looked down towards the beach again. Two young men had joined her and her blonde friend, and, though the other girl had her own claim to beauty in a tall, shapely figure, it was evident which one held the boys' attention.

Yet, watching her, Ryan saw no sign of any deliberate effort to do so. Her manner seemed friendly without being flirtatious. When she smiled, it was with a quick, engaging grin, dimpling her cheeks and making her look not much older than the photograph he had of her, taken several years earlier.

Apparently Lauren James also noticed the girl's lack of outward sophistication as she commented, 'Mind you, she still looks pretty much a kid. Certainly not what you'd expect with Rhea Cormack for a mother.'

'Oh, looks can be deceptive,' Stella said knowingly, 'and in some respects she's more like Rhea than one might imagine.'

'Mm, I can see she's popular. That's Dale's son, isn't it?'

'The one staring at her with doglike devotion, yes... But I wasn't really referring to those boys. I've reason to believe her main interest lies elsewhere. Very much *en famille*, as it were,' Stella said on a note inviting speculation.

'Someone Rhea was linked with...' Lauren deduced correctly, then pointed out, 'That leaves a pretty wide field, by all accounts.'

'I suppose it does,' Stella conceded with a hard laugh before hinting, 'What if I narrow it down to another award winner—a certain English actor turned director?'

'You don't mean...?' Lauren's eyes widened as the name on her lips was confirmed with a slow nod. 'Where *do* you get your information from? Obviously Jay Rutherford and Rhea worked together on *Sunset Gold*, but I wasn't aware they had a thing going.'

'Oh, it was long before that,' Stella said dismissively. 'As far back as when Rhea first came out to the West Coast, so I've been told. And they were very discreet about it, too. But apparently they lived together—oh, for years—in some beach-house near Santa Monica.'

'Really?' Lauren was suitably impressed by this fresh item of gossip. 'But why the secrecy? After all, Rhea was quite open about her other affairs.'

'*She* could afford to be,' asserted Stella. 'It was Jay who was married at the time and, being Catholic, likely to remain so.'

'I'd heard his first wife died of some awful nerve disease,' Lauren recalled with a frown.

'She did, but that was some years on,' Stella explained. 'At the time, she was stuck away in a sanatorium, and Jay could scarcely advertise the fact that he was shacking up with Rhea. It might have ruined his career, particularly with him always playing "men of integrity" roles.'

Lauren gave an understanding nod. 'Yes, it can be a drag, living up to your screen image. Of course, now he's directing, Jay must be able to do pretty much as he likes.'

'It would seem so. He certainly hasn't gone to any great lengths to hide his friendship with our little nymphet down there.'

'Why? Are they actually living together?'

'In a rented villa behind La Turbie,' Stella confirmed with a smug smile, before qualifying, 'At least, one assumes they still are, although the girl was notably absent from the awards ceremony.'

'Yes, Jay picked up Rhea's as well as his own, didn't he?' Lauren inserted. 'Perhaps that implies the daughter wasn't overfond of her famous mother.'

'Mm, could be,' Stella said in a thoughtful tone as she glanced down at the girl now slipping shorts and T-shirt over her swimsuit. 'At any rate, there has to be something distinctly odd about a young girl who sleeps with her mother's old lovers—the emphasis being decidedly on the *old*. I mean, attractive as Jay is, he must be on the wrong side of fifty.'

'It's quite an age gap,' Lauren agreed. 'Mind you, if she's planning on following in Rhea's footsteps, he could do a lot to help her career.'

'True,' Stella murmured as she watched the girls now climbing up the steps from the beach. 'Well, here she comes. I'd better say hello. After all, I *was* a good friend of her mother's,' she claimed, without the slightest trace of a blush.

Three pairs of eyes were trained on the doorway when the girls made their entrance. Kelly Cormack, however, barely noticed the man, and spared only a passing glance for the two women, before heading for a table at the opposite end of the room.

Her friend giggled as they sat down. 'I think you just snubbed the lovely Stella.'

'Did I?' came the shrugged reply.

And Suzie Bryant looked even more impressed with such nonchalance, confiding, 'She's poison, you know.'

'Oh, I know,' Kelly raised green eyes, holding a glint of mischief. 'Mother once said that if a rattlesnake bit

Stella Martin, it would be debatable who keeled over first.'

'I love it!' Suzie laughed in appreciation and, without thinking, added, 'Rhea was priceless, wasn't she?'

'Yes, *she was*,' her daughter confirmed, but on a more aggressive note, as though she expected someone to contradict it.

Suzie knew better. Like most people, she'd read the stories in the Press that suggested Rhea Cormack had been anything but 'priceless' in certain respects. She took her attitude from her friend, however, and Kelly had made it plain she wasn't going to apologise for her mother's past to anyone.

'*Mesdemoiselles?*' The waiter coughed discreetly to attract their attention, but, when one of the girls turned her head, his fixed smile became a spontaneous grin. 'Ah, Mademoiselle Kelly, *comment allez-vous?*'

'*Très bien,*' Kelly smiled back. '*Et vous?*'

'*Comme ci, comme ça.*' The young man hunched his shoulders in an expansive gesture, then, eyes twinkling, suggested, 'You wish the banana split, *non?*'

'*Oui,*' Kelly replied as expected, not having the heart to tell him she'd been about to order a plain orange juice.

She'd been coming to the Arbois every summer since she was fourteen. This year she'd stayed elsewhere, yet all the staff seemed to remember her—and, less fortunately, her childhood tastes.

The waiter flashed her another smile before finally taking notice of Suzie. 'And you, *mademoiselle?*'

'I thought you'd never ask,' she muttered drily, and, after he'd departed with her order, demanded of Kelly, 'Just tell me how you do it, girl?'

'Do what?' Kelly echoed.

Sighing expressively, Suzie enlarged, 'Waiters smile at her without a tip on their mind. Boys compete for her attention as if she was *the* only pebble on the beach. Even my odious brother Simon is a little less odious in her presence... And she says, *"Do what?"* '

Suzie raised her eyes heavenward, and Kelly laughed aloud.

'You're exaggerating—as usual,' she eventually said, only to have it denied moments later when their ices appeared, in record time and with yet another brilliant smile from the young waiter.

'Exaggerating, am I?' Suzie countered smugly when they'd been served. Then, with a spoonful of ice-cream suspended en route to her mouth, added almost dreamily, 'Isn't he lovely? He's a real strong and silent type.'

'The waiter?' Kelly said in surprise.

'No, stupid—my Australian!'

'Oh, *him*.' Kelly had no need to ask who Suzie's Australian was. She'd been talking about him down on the beach, and possibly he accounted for her insistence they have a last cold drink together in the hotel. 'Where is he?'

'Don't look!' Suzie whispered when Kelly made to turn. 'He's facing this way.'

'All right, I won't.' Kelly felt quite able to contain her curiosity.

'OK, you can look,' Suzie allowed, 'but don't *look*—if you know what I mean.'

'And I thought I was the crazy one,' Kelly laughed, before letting her napkin slip from her lap, and casually leaning down to retrieve it. On the way up, she glanced sideways to the man seated in the far corner, and formed the vaguest impression of blond hair and dark sunglasses.

'Well?' Suzie prompted.

'He's . . . nice,' she offered somewhat lamely.

'*Nice*?' was repeated in disgust. 'That's all you can say about that beautiful man—*nice*?'

Kelly shrugged. 'Well, at the risk of being totally unoriginal, I could also say you shouldn't judge a book by its cover.'

'*And* totally boring,' Suzie commented on this piece of homespun philosophy, but then admitted with a sigh, 'I suppose you're right, though. I should have learned looks aren't everything. What with the fool I made of myself over Antoine.'

Kelly pulled a face at the name. 'Forget him, Suz.'

'I can't—not after what happened,' Suzie went on mournfully. 'I mean, if I'd listened to you in the first place, I'd never have agreed to meet him at that crummy hotel in Lucerne.'

Kelly shook her head, denying any regret over answering her friend's distress call. She'd arrived at the backstreet hotel to find Suzie in a hysterical state, the bruises on her body revealing she'd been all but raped by the young Swiss. And later, when they'd been caught climbing through a window of their finishing school, she had tried to protect Suzie by taking the blame for missing curfew.

Unfortunately the school principal had not accepted the excuse offered and, insisting on a search of their handbags, had discovered the receipt for the hotel bill in Kelly's. Of course she had immediately leapt to the right conclusion about the wrong girl.

'It really wasn't your fault, Suzie,' she reassured once more, then reminded with a wry smile, 'At any rate, I think I can take the credit for my expulsion. You have to admit I managed that by my own efforts.'

'Perhaps.' Suzie smiled, too, as she thought of that confrontation with Madame Brunel. Dumbstruck at the time, she now ran on, 'I couldn't decide whether I wanted to cheer or sink through the floor when you told Madame what you thought of her and her lousy school. I never knew you had such a magnificent temper.'

'Neither did I,' Kelly confided with a short laugh.

'I just wish I hadn't been so spineless, letting you carry the can for me,' Suzie added, shamefaced at the way she'd acted. 'But the thought of my mother, finding about Antoine even when I hadn't . . . well, you know she'd never have believed me.'

Kelly nodded in sympathy, aware that Carol Bryant was not the most tolerant of parents. Certainly she would not have behaved as Kelly's own mother had, accepting her word that on the fatal evening she'd been helping an anonymous friend—and nothing else.

'Look, stop worrying!' Kelly said when Suzie's face remained mournful. 'In a way, things actually worked out for the best. At least I was able to spend more time with Mum.'

'I suppose so.' Suzie wasn't entirely convinced. 'But it hasn't helped your university plans, has it? If you'd graduated from the Academy, then maybe you wouldn't have had to sit that entrance exam at Easter.'

'I wouldn't be too sure.' Kelly suspected the University of Sorbonne would not have been over-impressed with a certificate from the Brunel Academy for Young Ladies. 'Anyway, if I haven't passed the entrance, it just means I'm not really good enough for the course.'

'Oh, you'll have passed.' Suzie had no doubts on that score. 'You're so brilliant at languages, how could you fail?'

'Thanks,' Kelly grinned at this extravagant compliment and kept quiet about her own doubts.

'So what have you decided to do till university starts?' Suzie went on to ask.

'Carry on keeping house for Jay, I think,' Kelly replied, an idea which prompted her to glance at her watch. 'Heavens, is that the time?'

'It's only four.' Suzie shrugged, but Kelly was already gathering her things together.

'I must run. Jay's probably awake by this time and expecting me back,' she explained.

'*Awake?*' Suzie echoed as she trailed her to the hotel lobby. 'You mean, he might still be in bed? My God, even my mother manages to surface by lunch time. If you ask me, I'd say Jay must paint the town a pretty vivid shade of red.'

'Then you'd be wrong,' Kelly retorted smartly. 'As it happens, he spent the night working on his next script, and didn't go to bed till eight in the morning. So he's entitled to sleep in,' she concluded on a defensive note.

But, if she anticipated any further comment on Jay's life-style, none was forthcoming. They'd reached the car park and Suzie was too busy staring at the motorbike beside which Kelly had halted.

'That *monster's* not yours?' she almost screeched.

'No, of course not,' Kelly denied, and, just as the other girl was breathing a sigh of relief, added, 'It came with the villa.'

'Jay *lets* you use that... *that thing*?' Suzie asked, pointing at the offending object—a powerful-looking five hundred cc Yamaha.

'Not exactly,' Kelly admitted, 'but I don't imagine he'll mind. I'm allowed to use the Mercedes normally, except today I couldn't find the keys, so I thought—why not try out the bike?' she finished with a shrug.

'I can think of a dozen good reasons,' Suzie stated half-seriously.

But Kelly took little notice, already straddling the heavy bike. 'Don't worry, it works much the same as my Honda. You don't even have to kick-start it. Just switch on... See?'

Suzie saw, but the horror on her face did not diminish as she shrieked above the engine's roar, 'Hell's teeth, Kelly, it sounds like Concorde on take-off! Are you sure you can handle it?'

'Oh, I won't go fast or anything,' Kelly replied and, pushing the bike off its stand, made a wide circle around her friend to display the fact she could handle it.

Impressed, but not wholly convinced, Suzie shouted, 'Give us a call when you get back to the villa.'

'OK!' Kelly shouted back, and departed with a last grin.

Neither girl had observed their audience, Ryan Devlin, standing in the hotel doorway. He'd arrived in time to watch Kelly circling the car park, his expression rigid with disbelief. A moment sooner and he'd have acted on his first impulse—to drag her bodily off the massive bike. As it was, he strode towards his hire-car, angry eyes slicing straight through Suzie, who offered him a tentative smile in passing.

Then he powered the BMW up the driveway after the bike—only to see no sign of it from the top gates. He was left to assume she was going to La Turbie, the village mentioned by one of the actresses. He knew from touring the area that it lay in the hills behind Monaco and, with a quick glance at the map, he decided to head for the twisting backroad that climbed to the Grande Corniche, the highest route skirting the Côte d'Azur.

Delayed by traffic in Beaulieu, he was some miles up the hill road, and about to admit defeat, when he finally spotted the bike, disappearing round a bend. Any sense of satisfaction faded, however, as he drew closer. For, in spite of some evidence of skill in her cornering, she didn't look much bigger than a child on the black and chrome machine. So slight, it seemed the wind flapping at her jacket might easily blow her over, and, bare-headed and barelegged, she wouldn't stand a chance if that happened.

For sheer irresponsibility, Ryan decided the girl could only be matched by whoever permitted her such a dangerous toy. Coupling it with her obviously reckless nature, he wouldn't have allowed her within a mile of it if she'd been under his care.

If...or when? The question brought a twist to Ryan's lips as he recognised a certain hypocrisy behind his thoughts. In theory, he had travelled over three continents, looking for this girl; in practice, he'd just gone through the motions, not wanting her found. Two days ago, when she'd not been at the Festival Hall in Cannes to collect her mother's award, he had finally given up the search. Tomorrow he would have boarded a plane home without the slightest qualm.

And now?

Ryan swore under his breath, wishing he had walked out of the conservatory the moment he'd heard Rhea Cormack's name. But he hadn't. And, though more than ever he believed the past better buried, it was no longer possible to simply return to Australia, claiming he'd never found her.

So he stayed on her tail as they climbed to the Grande Corniche, debating his next move and wondering what kind of girl chose to live with some ageing film director.

Not the sweet little girl visualised by the man who'd sent him to find her. Of that, Ryan was sure.

Meanwhile, Kelly had no suspicion she was being followed.

If she noticed the white BMW occasionally appearing in her wing mirror, she was more concerned about the cars which actually overtook her. She'd been using a bike to get round the busy Riviera roads for the last two summers, and the powerful Yamaha did handle basically the same as smaller models. Unfortunately, other motorists seemed to expect her to go faster on it, and showed their impatience, either by passing in awkward places, or by whizzing by so close she had to hug the low perimeter wall, beyond which lay a steep drop.

Kelly was already making her own mind up that this would be her first and last jaunt on the big bike, when the decision was taken from her.

The accident happened as she came wide out of a bend to discover, of all things, a mountain goat strolling down the centre of the road. Her first instinct was to veer to the right, and undoubtedly that would have smashed the bike into the boundary wall before sending her headlong over the hillside. Instead, the startled animal beat her to it and she had to swerve across the road, the screech of brakes echoing the silent screaming in her head as she careered towards the opposite hillface.

It had taken only seconds.

The BMW rounded the corner moments later, already too late for its driver to do anything, other than take in the scene. The road was now empty, with no sign of what might have caused the accident. But up ahead, at the end of a gravel lay-by, its results were evident.

Ryan pulled into the lay-by, well short of girl and bike, then went on foot to check the absolute stillness of both. He came within five yards, close enough to confirm his first impressions.

She was lying on her back, body pinned by the bike, head tilted towards the sky. Her eyes were open, glazed with an expression that denied anything tragic. But death had many forms, and once Ryan had seen a man thrown from his horse and break his back, then die very quietly, with the exact same look of contentment on his face.

A peaceful image, yet this time Ryan had to quell a strong wave of nausea before he turned away to fetch his jacket from the car. Knowing he shouldn't move her, he wanted to at least cover her face. Still lovely, it was too stark a reminder that, no matter what kind of girl she'd been, Rhea Cormack's daughter had not even reached her twentieth birthday.

CHAPTER TWO

KELLY found it a strange feeling, as though her mind
was floating somewhere above her body. Experiencing
no pain, yet never so conscious of the world around
her—the cloudless blue of the summer sky and the sweet
scents in the air. As if she'd died and gone to heaven,
she thought, only on a note of pure joy because she most
definitely hadn't.

She still couldn't quite believe it. Less than a foot from
the hillside and she'd turned the bike out of that skid.
Bare inches as the brakes locked and the tyres threw up
a spray of gravel. She'd even managed to stand for a
second before the weight of the bike toppled her over.
But she knew it was sheer luck that she'd escaped without
a scratch.

Well, perhaps not altogether. She grimaced slightly as
she became conscious of the scraped skin on her leg
where she'd fallen hard. In a moment she'd wriggle out
from under the bike and inspect the damage to both of
them. The pain, however, did not diminish that sense
of wonder in being alive—a wonder which glazed her
wide, green eyes as she lay, staring up at the skies above.

In that state of detachment, Kelly didn't hear the car
or Ryan's footsteps the first time he approached. Only
later, when he was near enough to cast a shadow, did
she come back to earth to register his presence. And,
finding her light blocked out by a tall, looming figure,
she slanted her head to one side.

The slightest of movements, it seemed to have a dra-
matic effect on the man, his breath rasping harshly as
he jerked back a pace.

Puzzled, Kelly raised herself on to her elbows and read
the shock in his expression. Then she noticed the jacket

he held out, as if he were going to cover something. It took her a couple seconds to grasp what the something was, and she reacted spontaneously.

Kelly's laughter was a clear, light-hearted sound which normally drew a similar response. On this occasion, however, it drew a rigid stare.

Realising her amusement wasn't shared, Kelly made a creditable effort to control it, but another laugh escaped, transforming the stare into a grim frown. So she clamped her lips tightly shut and managed to convert the next one into a cough. Only that didn't meet the stranger's approval either, as the frown became a deepening scowl.

No sense of humour, Kelly concluded, her own finally sobering.

'I'm sorry. Perhaps I shouldn't have laughed, but you see, I'm not dead.' She paused, reconsidered her words and, with a wry grimace, ran on, 'That was silly of me. Of course you can see I'm not dead. What I mean is, I was laughing because I was so pleased to find I wasn't... Dead, that is. I'm not hurt, either. Well, only super-ficially—a few scratches maybe, not worth mentioning...'

Eventually Kelly trailed off, her smile slipping as all it received in return was a look that suggested total incomprehension. Then it occurred to her she had automatically spoken in English, which he might not understand. So she tried again in French, in view of where they were, and, when that elicited no response, switched to Italian, at which point he finally interrupted.

'Before you go through your whole repertoire, I think I can cope with your English... just about,' he stated, in what was clearly his first language, too.

Faintly irritated, Kelly asked, 'Why didn't you say so, then?'

But the question was ignored as he bent down to lift the bike off her legs, on to its stand, and, though he offered a hand when she started to rise, his expression could hardly be termed friendly.

Still, Kelly felt she should be showing some gratitude. 'Thanks very much for stopping. And I really am sorry for laughing, but I was——'

'Yes, I know. You told me,' Ryan cut in, wanting to spare himself another of her explanations. On performance so far, he had yet to decide if Miss Kelly Cormack was odd in the head or just plain stupid.

He let his eyes run over her, inspecting for damage, and frowned when he reached the scratches scoring her thigh. Painful, he would imagine, but she seemed unconcerned, more intent on dusting down her jacket and shorts. A tough little thing, Ryan had to give her that, if nothing else.

His grey eyes shifted to the bike as he asked, 'Is this death contraption yours?'

'Sort of,' Kelly shrugged, and, sensing a lecture imminent, decided it was time to go. 'Well, I mustn't keep you. Thanks again.' She straddled her uninjured leg over the bike.

The action was awarded a stunned stare, followed by an incredulous, 'You're not still thinking of riding that machine?'

'Looks like it,' she said with a mildly impudent smile. 'I mean, if I wait around, I might lose my nerve. They say it's best if you climb back on immediately after you've had a fall.'

'That applies to horses, not bikes,' Ryan replied heavily, 'and even then, only when you know how to handle one in the first place.'

'*I do!*' Kelly claimed on an indignant note. 'This is the first accident I've ever had *and* it was scarcely my fault.'

'No?' He scanned the empty road.

'*It wasn't!*' she insisted. 'When I came round the bend, there was a mountain goat in the middle of the road. I had to swerve to avoid him.'

'A mountain goat?' he echoed in disbelief.

'*Yes*, it was grey and white, with a bell round its neck.' Kelly thought the description would give credence to her story.

It didn't. 'So where's Billy now?' Ryan enquired with a sceptical look, and, when she opened her mouth to reply, quickly added, 'Never mind. I'll take your word for it. Come on.'

Frowning, Kelly watched him pocket the key of the bike before announcing, 'I'll give you a lift to wherever you were going.'

Not the most gracious offer she'd ever had, she barely hesitated in refusing it. 'Thanks all the same, but I can't leave the bike here. It belongs to the villa my friend's renting.'

'Then your *friend* can collect it, can't he?' Ryan suggested shortly.

'I wouldn't think so.' Kelly shook her head over the unlikely image of a suave, comfort-loving Jay on the motorbike. 'In any case, I've only a few miles to go, and I promise I'll be dead careful,' she said with a winning smile.

It was totally wasted on Ryan, as he drawled back, 'It's the dead part that worries me.'

And, frustrated, Kelly almost snapped, 'Look, I'll be fine.'

'Forget it,' Ryan dismissed, his patience also running out. 'Either you let me drive you home, or you walk. Take your pick!'

But, if that was intended to conclude the argument, Kelly was only beginning to get into her stride. 'I can always stick out a thumb and hitch a ride, you know.'

'You'd accept a lift from a complete stranger?' In his disgust, Ryan failed to see any contradiction.

Kelly didn't. 'You don't think that's advisable?' she asked, her voice deceptively innocent, and, at the exasperated sigh it drew, agreed, 'No, I suppose not. Strangers can be a bit odd. Of course, that also means

I can't really accept your kind offer of a lift, either...
Can I?'

It took Ryan a moment to understand her thinly veiled
sarcasm, then he growled back, 'Ryan Devlin.'

Kelly looked at him blankly.

'That's my name—Ryan Devlin,' he repeated, before
stiffly announcing, 'And I can assure you, Miss
Cormack, you haven't the slightest reason to fear
any... any *advances* from me.'

With that scowl permanently etched on his face, Kelly
hadn't even considered the possibility. His use of her
surname, however, did warrant a suspicious frown. 'You
know who I am?'

'I'm staying at the Arbois. You were pointed out to
me earlier,' Ryan admitted, a very limited explanation
of the truth.

But Kelly accepted it and the coincidence of their
meeting, though she commented astutely enough, 'As
Rhea Cormack's daughter, I suppose.'

'Yes,' he nodded. 'Why? Does that bother you?'

'Not terribly,' she shrugged. 'I'm used to it. I can
probably guess what your friends said.'

'And what would that be?' he prompted.

'Oh, something about being nothing like my mother.
That's usually what people say, because they expect me
to be a tall, beautiful redhead instead of... well, dark
and small,' she grimaced, as if neither could be considered an attribute.

Ryan stared back at her in surprise. Still perched on
the motorbike, she was indeed very slight, her figure
more like a slim boy's in the sports clothes she wore.
Yet, in her own way, with the dark curls and the con-
trasting green eyes, she was as striking as the mother
had been. What surprised him was the fact she didn't
seem to know it.

'Was I right, then?' she challenged on an amused note.

'More or less.' Momentarily, Ryan forgot the other things said about her, and found himself responding to the quick grin he was offered.

When he smiled instead of scowling, Kelly also realised Ryan might be classed as an attractive man. Indeed, with his handsome, if slightly severe, features and his tall, rangy build, she decided somewhat facetiously that he would be perfect casting for the strong, silent type.

Then it struck her who had planted such a hackneyed phrase in her mind—who had used it that very afternoon. And all at once she made the connection between his dark blond looks, his drawling accent, and the fact he was staying at the Arbois.

'Suzie's Australian!' she exclaimed without thinking.

Fortunately his, 'What?' suggested that, if he'd caught her words, he was having a problem making sense of them.

She added quickly, 'I said you're Australian.'

'True,' he agreed, smiling a little, before he brought them right back to the original argument by asking, 'Is that in my favour or not—as far as accepting a lift goes?'

Kelly held in a sigh. 'Look, it's not that I don't trust you. In fact, I'm sure you think you're acting in my best interests.'

'I'm pleased to have your confidence.'

'But,' she continued, ignoring his sarcasm, 'surely you can see I'll have to get the bike back to the villa somehow?'

His impassive expression at first suggested the appeal was lost on him. Then he glanced down at the bike and asked on a note of compromise, 'After it's back, you won't use it again?'

'Never, cross my heart,' she agreed readily.

Too readily, she decided, from the sceptical look she was given, but after a moment's consideration, he held out a leather key-ring to her. She took it quickly, before noticing the maker's badge.

'You've given me the wrong one.' She offered the key back with a smile.

He shook his head. 'I'm going to ride the bike, you drive the car,' he informed her.

Then, as if that settled the matter, he placed a hand on her arm and indicated she should climb off the bike.

Aware he could easily pull her off, Kelly decided to get down voluntarily. But, once on solid ground, she muttered, 'I don't think this is such a hot idea.'

What she thought, however, was obviously not of the slightest interest to him. Without even sparing her a glance, he straddled the bike and lifting it, kicked the stand away.

Almost a foot taller than Kelly, he had no problems balancing the bike. She was scowling over the fact when he finally took notice of her again.

'You can drive, can't you?'

'Yes, of course! I take it you know how to ride a bike?' she retorted in kind.

It earned her a direct stare, if not an answer. A warning stare, she decided, before he suggested heavily, 'Just lead the way. OK?'

'OK,' she muttered back and, without another word, turned on her heel.

She'd barely reached the car when he started revving up the bike. Taking it as a sign of impatience, she decided not to waste any more of his time, and hastily strapped herself behind the driving wheel to turn on the car engine. She also wanted to prove herself a good driver, but in trying to indicate her intention of pulling out, she managed instead to set the wipers swishing. Flustered by this mistake, she followed it up by switching them to 'fast' before finding 'off' again. She glanced up to check if her incompetence was being witnessed, and felt absolutely no surprise to find it was. Too far away to actually read his expression, she could imagine the exasperation written on it.

Muttering to herself, she made quite sure it was the indicator she clicked on next, then, checking an inordinate number of times in her mirror, she pulled out of the lay-by to the far side of the road. When she passed by him at an over-cautious crawl, he gave her a nod that just might have been meant as reassuring, and waited till she was some yards ahead before following.

After the first mile, she gradually lost her nervousness of the unfamiliar car, its steering not being dissimilar to Jay's Mercedes. And, though she remained conscious of the Australian behind her, it began to seem rather silly to feel he was watching and criticising her every move. Mostly he kept his distance on the twisting hillroad and, when she did glimpse him in her wing-mirror, he looked quite relaxed about the whole thing, possibly even enjoying the bike ride. She had to admit, however grudgingly, he handled the Yamaha with a good deal more confidence than she did.

When they reached La Turbie, he closed the gap between them and stayed on her tail as she took a secondary road into the hills behind, before finally turning down the narrow access lane to the villa where she was staying.

Built on a plateau, the house and grounds were hidden behind a high wall to ensure privacy. At the end of the lane, Kelly climbed out of the car to open a set of gates and wave the Australian through. Then, leaving the gate wide for his departure, she followed on up the short driveway and turned the BMW to stand in the middle on the gravel forecourt, while he parked the bike by the garaging at the side.

The villa itself stood a few steps above, surrounded by a terrace of tropical plants. White-walled, with green shuttered windows, it was large enough to be impressive, even by Riviera standards.

Certainly, the Australian was staring hard up at it when Kelly joined him. 'Who owns this place?' he asked, dashing her hopes that he would leave immediately.

She did not have a chance to answer before the sound of a door opening distracted them both. She turned towards the villa to see Jason Rutherford, handsome and silver-haired, standing at a set of french windows by the terrace. Trusting the Australian would take the hint, she abandoned him without another word, and almost raced up the steps to greet the older man.

Smiling, Jay bent to kiss her cheek. 'I was just about to send out a search party. Suzie phoned ten minutes ago and seemed rather concerned that you weren't home.'

'I ... um ... had a little trouble with the bike,' she admitted hesitantly.

'The bike?' He looked blank.

'The one in the garage,' Kelly explained. 'I couldn't find the keys to the Merc, so I took it instead.'

This time Jay nodded and, obviously ready to drop the subject, directed a politely enquiring smile somewhere beyond her shoulder. It made Kelly realise she'd been optimistic in imagining the Australian would simply depart of his own accord. She glanced round to find him standing at the top of the steps, then back at Jay, who gave her an expectant look.

'This is Ryan Devlin,' she felt obliged to say.

'How do you do? I'm Jay Rutherford.' Her half-hearted introduction was completed by Jay, stretching out his hand with a smile.

'Mr Rutherford.' Ryan stepped forward and briefly took the hand offered.

Another silence followed, while Jay waited for her to further identify the tall, blond stranger. Choosing the most irrelevant of details, she murmured, 'Mr Devlin's staying at the Arbois.'

'Oh, I see,' Jay remarked urbanely, but with a faintly teasing gleam in his eye that suggested he definitely did not see.

Kelly gave a slight shake of her head, trying to disclaim any kind of friendship with Ryan Devlin, while still hoping to avoid any discussion on the bike incident.

But she should have known better than to think the Australian would need a lead-up from her to broach the subject.

'We actually met on the road up here—after she'd had her accident on that bike,' he relayed grimly.

'*Accident?*' Jay repeated in shock. 'My God, love, are you hurt?' Anxious eyes winged back to her, searching for injury.

'No, I'm fine, Jay. Honestly.' She smiled reassuringly at the older man, before aiming a silencing glare elsewhere.

However, it was to no effect, for the Australian went on, 'She's cut up her leg quite badly.'

It had Jay crouching down to examine the gashes on her thigh, and agreeing, 'They *are* nasty. How did the accident happen?'

'A mountain goat in the middle of the road,' she recounted, another stare defying the Australian to contradict her.

But this time he remained silent, while Jay accepted her story with a mutter of, 'It's a damn nuisance, the way they're allowed to stray.'

And Kelly couldn't resist giving the Australian a superior 'told-you-so' look.

Unaware of the wordless message passing over his head, Jay straightened up to say, 'I don't think any of the cuts are deep enough to require stitches, but you'd better sterilise them.'

'Yes, I will.' Kelly had every intention of following this advice—as soon as Ryan Devlin departed.

Unfortunately, Jay misunderstood her reluctance to leave them alone, his smile teasing as he suggested, 'Why don't you go upstairs and do that now, while I fix Mr Devlin a drink?'

She almost groaned aloud and, waiting in vain for the Australian to turn down the invitation, prompted, 'Mr Devlin's in a hurry... aren't you?'

There was a noticeable pause, as if he was debating the matter, but he finally agreed, 'I'm afraid so, yes.'

'Oh, well...another time, perhaps.' Jay smiled politely, then, as the telephone began ringing inside, excused himself.

In no apparent hurry, Ryan Devlin stood staring after the older man. From his expression, something seemed to have surprised or puzzled him.

Deciding another hint was in order, Kelly said, 'I'll show you to your car,' and led the way back down the steps.

As they walked in silence towards the BMW, she found herself feeling both defensive and angry—suspecting she was behaving badly, but blaming the Australian for it. Every time he spoke to her, he seemed to breathe disapproval.

Once installed behind the steering wheel of his car, he looked askance at her through the open window. 'I hope you meant it—about not riding the bike again.'

Kelly's mouth set in a sullen line. 'As I remember, I promised not to, before we even arrived back here,' she pointed out. 'And you didn't have to go on like that to Jay. He's not responsible for what I do.'

'Obviously,' he agreed on a short, derisive note.

'Meaning?' she snapped in reply.

'*Meaning* it's damn plain the man has no control over you,' he ground out.

Scowling as she wondered how old he imagined her to be, Kelly demanded, 'Why should he have?'

'Someone needs to,' Ryan growled back as he switched on the engine and shoved the car into gear. Having concluded the argument, he pulled away and caught sight of her, pulling faces, in his rear-view mirror.

Someone, he added silently, but it sure as hell won't be me!

In that frame of mind, he drove back to the Arbois, and wasted no time in sending a telegram to Australia.

It read simply, 'Found her. Living with older man. Advise leave alone.'

Then he spent the whole evening trying to dismiss her from his mind. Only it proved irritatingly difficult—rather like trying to ignore a nagging toothache. Or, in this case, a smile—bright and innocent one moment, full of insolence the next. A contradictory image, it made him angry without really knowing why.

It was much the same for Kelly. While she prepared the evening meal at the villa, her mind kept straying back to their encounter. She recalled things he'd said, and vented her temper on pots and pans and cupboard doors. Then she imagined the things she *hadn't* said, but should have, especially at the end. And, when she finally produced a rather burnt-at-the-edges lasagne, she put the blame firmly on one bossy, overbearing Australian who didn't know when he wasn't wanted—even in a person's thoughts!

Jay didn't help, as he raised the subject over dinner, asking, 'By the way, who introduced you to that Australian?'

'No one, really,' Kelly replied. 'Suzie did point him out when I was at the Arbois, but I didn't take much notice at the time.'

'So how did you actually meet?'

'Oh, he came along after I'd fallen off the bike, and decided I needed rescuing.'

'That was a coincidence,' Jay frowned slightly. 'Him being at the Arbois, I mean, then turning up on the same stretch of road later.'

'I suppose,' Kelly agreed, though she hadn't considered the coincidence that remarkable.

'You don't think he might have been following you, do you?'

'Following me? Why ever should he do that?'

Jay hesitated, as if about to say something serious, but in the end he just smiled, and remarked lightly, 'Because you're a beautiful girl, of course.'

'Oh, of course,' Kelly echoed. 'I suppose that's why he treated me like a not-very-bright ten-year-old.'

'Did he really?'

'Yes, he did, and it wasn't that funny.'

The last was a warning to Jay, who was looking amused as well as curious. He didn't altogether take heed, a smile still creasing his eyes, but he didn't ask any more questions about the Australian.

Instead he resumed his meal, and switched to talking of his next film, set in Egypt and due to begin shooting the following week. Though she had no aspirations to be an actress, Kelly listened with interest as he recounted a few of the last-minute problems that had cropped up.

It was much later, when Kelly was on the point of retiring to bed, that Jay resurrected the subject. 'For the record, did your Australian say what he did for a living?'

'No. Why?' Kelly couldn't see the significance of such a detail.

'Just wondering,' he dismissed, almost too casually.

That was when an awful thought struck her. 'You don't suppose he's some kind of reporter, do you?'

'Reporter?' Clearly the idea had never crossed Jay's mind. 'I doubt it. Not the type.'

'Are you sure?' Kelly's face was clouded with anxiety.

'Quite,' Jay stressed, at the same time giving her a comforting hug. 'So don't start worrying about that again.'

'All right.' Kelly smiled back and, kissing his cheek, left him to his night's work.

Once in bed, however, she did start worrying. What if Ryan Devlin *was* a reporter? Admittedly, he didn't seem the type. But if Jay was right—and he had been following her—couldn't that be the reason? Recalling her past experience of the Press, she desperately hoped not.

After the car crash, reporters had appeared like a pack of vultures, picking over the details of her mother's life. It had been difficult not to let the stories hurt—and, worse, impossible to dismiss them all as fiction.

For, if Kelly defended her mother, it was out of love, not ignorance. She knew too well that Rhea Cormack, the film star, had gone from man to man in search of a happiness that would last.

The first had been Armand Duval, a director of note and Kelly's father. How they'd met wasn't clear, but he had taken a raw, young Irish girl and turned her into a major name of the French cinema. He'd also lived with her for the remaining years of his life.

Kelly had been six when he had died, but she still had a good memory of a tall, grey-haired man, with laughing eyes and a gentle manner. As a child, she had accepted their relationship without question. It was much later when she discovered her mother had never actually married him, for the simple, terrible reason that he already had a wife.

History had repeated itself when they moved to America. Then it had been Jay—also Catholic, also married. They lived with him for four years, until she was twelve, and she took it for granted that he was 'officially' her stepfather.

When the affair ended, it had a shattering effect on Kelly. Unlike the children of many celebrities, she had been given an almost conventional upbringing. Living in relative seclusion in Spanish California, she'd attended a private day-school which, if not rigidly strict, gave sound instruction in the Catholic faith. Against this background, she could not fail to be appalled by the idea her mother had been 'living in sin' with Jay.

After that, they had moved to a white-brick mansion in Beverly Hills. A lavish showplace, it did not seem a real home to Kelly. She preferred the simplicity of their Spanish villa and, despite everything, badly missed Jay. Her school was very different, too. Though bright, she felt years behind the worldly wise Hollywood teenagers. In many ways, she was.

Eventually Rhea Cormack had recognised her daughter wasn't settling into their new life and, in realising why, had not wished her to lose the very naïveté that set her apart. Committed to a succession of films, however, she'd been unable to leave Hollywood at the time. So she'd sent Kelly to stay with her grandmother in Ireland.

Kelly knew that it wasn't in any sense a rejection, more an act of love by a woman often lonely in success. And if this 'temporary' arrangement had lasted several years, it was at her choosing. For she'd found herself more at home in a small fishing village in County Clare than the sunnier climes of California.

Almost from the start, she'd been popular with the local children. While boasting of her famous mother would have had an adverse effect, her very reticence had acted in her favour. And, though the villagers never quite came to regard her as one of them, most agreed that, despite being Rhea Cormack's 'child of shame', she was a remarkably nice girl.

Of course, in a staunchly Catholic country, Kelly couldn't help becoming conscious of her illegitimacy. On occasion, her own aunt had cast the fact up to her. That was until Granny Cormack caught her at it and, with a few well chosen words, showed whose side she was on.

A quirky old lady who believed in speaking her mind, Bridget Cormack treated Kelly with an indulgence never accorded the rest of the family. The Irish temper, that flared at the smallest offence from anyone else, was used to protect her 'special' grandchild. And, in return, Kelly grew to love her grandmother, and was probably the most grief-stricken when she died.

Just turned eighteen, she was immediately whisked away from Ballycove by Rhea and enrolled in an exclusive Swiss finishing school. It was her mother's wish that Kelly would gain entry into society circles, finer and grander than the film world.

At the time, Kelly wasn't sure if she wanted to be 'polished' and turned into a 'young lady'. But she was equally uncertain about the alternative—returning to live in Hollywood.

It wasn't that she'd stopped loving her mother. In spite of their separation, they'd remained close, with Rhea scheduling her career so they were together for most school holidays. Those months had been exclusively Kelly's. But over the years rumours had filtered back to Ireland about her mother's involvement with a series of male co-stars and, if outwardly Kelly had written it all off as publicity, she didn't want to put herself in the position of finding out differently.

So she went to Madame Brunel's, and discovered it really wasn't that bad. Well liked by most of the other girls, she'd made a particular friend of Suzie, whose producer father had recommended the school to Rhea.

She'd been halfway through a second year when her expulsion had forced her return to America. Yet she had no real regrets. For those last few months with her mother had left only pleasant memories.

Joining her in Mexico, on the location set of *Sunset Gold*, she had seen firsthand what a fine, professional actress Rhea Cormack was. And, if her mother had seemed to be growing very friendly with its director, Kelly hadn't minded—not when the director was Jay Rutherford. In fact, she had positively conspired to get them back together, knowing that Jay was now a widower and his intentions went beyond an affair.

Perhaps her mother would have finally married him, perhaps not. Kelly had hoped so, because Jay seemed likely to make her happy. But, either way, it would not have mattered.

During those final months, Kelly had learned to accept her mother for the person she was. She might not wish to be just like her—in one important respect she intended to be as unlike her as possible—but, regardless of what was written or said, Kelly stubbornly refused to let it change her feelings.

In the end, she still loved the funny, lovely lady of her childhood.

She always would.

CHAPTER THREE

THREE days later, Ryan was still waiting for a reply to his telegram—and still hoping it would contain the answer he wanted. Having little else to occupy his mind, he'd gone over his meeting with the girl, only to strengthen a conviction that she was bad news. Perhaps not quite the self-centred, empty-headed Hollywood brat he'd expected, but if she had an odd kind of charm he imagined it would prove as destructive as her mother's.

Certainly, in one brief encounter, she'd managed to provoke his normally cool temper more times than he cared to admit. He also felt he'd learned enough about her to know she could never be transplanted to a hot, dusty cattle station in the middle of nowhere. Nor was it remotely likely that she'd agree to go. So there seemed little point in another meeting.

The decision, however, was taken from him, that same afternoon, when the reply finally came. Its message was simple—bring her back.

Not the answer he'd wanted at all. Yet he accepted his father's wishes with resignation, then began wondering how he was meant to persuade Kelly Cormack to return with him to the other side of the world. At present, she'd probably cross the street just to avoid him. And would she be any more amenable when he told her the truth?

Somehow he doubted it, but now there seemed little point in delaying a second meeting. So once more he took the tortuous backroad up to La Turbie, and arrived mid-afternoon to find the villa gates shut, but unlocked.

He decided to leave his car in the lane outside and walk up the driveway. He saw the garage was open and empty, except for the motorbike. It seemed at least one of the villa occupants had gone out somewhere.

He mounted the terrace steps to pause in front of the french doors leading into the lounge. A glance revealed the room was unoccupied, but he noticed the windows on the far side were thrown wide. He skirted round the path to the rear of the villa.

The back terrace also proved deserted, a couple of empty glasses left on the patio table. And, apart from the usual clicking of crickets in the surrounding bushes, there was an almost unnatural quiet about the place.

Ryan raised his eyes to the balcony above without catching any signs of life. Then he turned his back on the house and walked towards a gap in the patio hedging. Beyond it, he discovered the luxury of a swimming pool.

Coming out at the top end, Ryan cast a quick glance down its considerable length. Not really expecting anyone to be there, he was arrested by the sight of the girl, stretched out on a sunlounger at the side. From her relaxed pose, eyes closed to the sun, he knew instantly that she was alone in the villa—and every instinct of good sense told him to back away quietly without announcing his presence.

But he was held there, staring at her body in unwilling fascination. For it seemed her modesty on the hotel beach did not extend to the privacy of this villa—nor did her near-nakedness reveal the childish figure he'd first imagined.

Though her legs and bikini-clad hips might be slender, any impression of immaturity faded the moment his eyes were drawn to her breasts. Oiled a glistening, naked, golden brown, they were beautifully shaped, firm and perfectly rounded. If a slightly lighter tan than the rest of her body, the difference in skin colour only served to emphasise their fullness, as did the dark, dusky areolae at their peak.

After a week at the Arbois, Ryan had thought he'd grown immune to women parading around topless. When he realised how hard he was staring at the girl's body and felt his own beginning to respond, it came as a shock. He stared for a moment longer, trying to deny the effect she had on him, then tore his eyes away.

Perhaps she was lovely enough to evoke a similar reaction from most men, but Kelly Cormack was the last girl on earth he should want in that way. The very idea disgusted him. Yet still his eyes were drawn once more to her as she stirred.

Possibly some sixth sense had warned Kelly she was being watched. If so, it was Jason Rutherford she expected to see as she blinked sleepily against the hazy sunlight and brought in focus the figure at the far end of the pool.

Startled fully awake, she sat bolt upright in the lounger, forgetting her state of undress. But she was abruptly reminded of it by the male eyes shifting momentarily from her indignant expression to the swell of her breasts. She snatched up a towel to shield herself, and wavered between embarrassment and fury.

'What do you want?' She meant to sound imperious, but it came out nervous.

The question was ignored anyway as he asked, 'Where's Rutherford?'

'He's out,' she scowled back, before realising it wasn't the smartest of admissions. 'But he'll be back soon... *very soon*,' she added with a warning ring.

Ryan recognised her fear and raised his hands in a placatory gesture. 'Look, I've come to talk. Nothing else.'

Kelly still shifted to the edge of her lounger, preparing for flight as she echoed, 'Talk? About what?'

Ryan halted some yards from her, searching for the best way to broach the subject. 'It's about your mother. Or at least something that happened in her past.'

'I see.' Fear left Kelly as contempt took its place. 'So that's who you really are.'

'You know?' Ryan hadn't anticipated that.

'Oh, I think so.' Her mouth curved with distaste. 'I mean, your approach might be a little more original, but your variety of reptile is still pretty easy to spot. The only question is which stone you crawled out from. Some trashy Australian magazine, I suppose.'

Ryan took a moment to understand exactly how he was being insulted, then he said incredulously, 'You think I'm a reporter?'

'Either that or some biography hack,' Kelly returned scornfully. 'But it doesn't matter which because I'm not going to talk about my mother. Not to you. Not now. Not ever!' she stated with angry emphasis.

It roused Ryan's curiosity, such that for an instant he forgot a denial and said instead, 'You really hated her, didn't you? You must have to feel this way.'

'Must I?' She gave a derisive laugh. 'Or isn't that just what *you* want to hear? How selfish she was, how cruel? Doesn't that make it a better story?'

'Is it true?' Ryan countered and, by doing so, confirmed his identity in Kelly's mind.

'If you must know, my mother was a kind, lovely, funny lady who always did her best for me,' she claimed fiercely. 'Not that I expect you to believe me, of course. After all, it wouldn't fit with the garbage you people have been writing about her. But you can be sure of this—if you print anything other than what I've just said, I'll sue you and your magazine blind,' she threatened on a last strident note.

By then, Ryan was standing with his hands on hips and an exaggerated expression of patience on his face.

He enquired, 'Are you quite finished?'

Recognising sarcasm, Kelly didn't answer, but her mouth compressed into a sullen line of dislike.

'Because if you are,' he continued, 'I might get the chance to tell you that I am not—and never have been—any variety of journalist. A fact you can easily verify from my passport,' he added, removing the book from his jacket pocket and coming a couple of steps closer to toss it on the lounger beside her.

Still hugging her towel, Kelly slid the passport a sideways glance, but made no move to pick it up. It was bad enough feeling she might just have jumped to one very wrong conclusion about him. She didn't particularly want the fact confirmed.

'Go ahead, check it!' he prompted.

'Why should I? It won't prove much,' she muttered sulkily. 'I mean, you can almost put what you like on a passport.

'God almighty, girl, do you always have to have smart answers to everything?' Ryan demanded, his patience slipping altogether.

Tempted to give a 'smart answer' in reply, Kelly confined herself to saying, 'I was merely stating a fact.'

'Then let me give you a couple,' he growled back. 'First, I have not the remotest interest in your mother's life story, however colourful it might be. And second, I don't appreciate being called a liar, particularly by some spoilt film star's brat... Got it?'

Kelly got it all right, every derisive word, but this time she didn't bother with an answer, smart or otherwise. Instead, she rose to her feet, threw him a last venomous glance and, before he could even guess at her intention, dropped the towel she was clutching to take a clean, neat dive into the pool. The gesture couldn't have been more rude or dismissive.

But when she surfaced at the far side, it was to find him still standing where she'd left him. Only now his face was a mask of barely controlled fury as he called over, 'You have exactly thirty seconds to get the hell out of there!'

'And if I don't? What are you going to do—come in after me?' she enquired with a scornful look.

'Twenty seconds,' was all the reply he gave.

Unintimidated, Kelly swam back to the middle of the pool and, treading water, advised tauntingly, 'You'd look pretty ridiculous, you know—returning to the Arbois dripping wet.'

'Twelve seconds,' he continued to count down with an accuracy of timing that began to worry her just a little.

'I'll tell you what,' she adopted a more bargaining tone, 'I'll accept you're not a reporter, if you take back that spoilt brat crack. Then we'll call it quits, OK?'

'Five seconds,' he warned as if he hadn't heard her. 'Are you coming out?'

'No, I'm not.' Kelly glared back at him in defiance.

And though he then started to unbutton the white cotton shirt he was wearing, she still didn't believe he meant to dive in after her. He was just trying to panic her. With some success, she had to admit, her eyes widening as he stripped off the shirt to reveal a smoothly muscled expanse of chest.

Noting this loss of confidence, Ryan suddenly found himself enjoying the situation. He draped his shirt over the lounger, then sat down to remove his shoes and socks. His actions were deliberate rather than hurried, but they had the desired effect as the girl watched him with an increasingly doubtful expression. Then he stood up and, holding her eyes, slowly unbuckled his belt.

'You'd better turn your back at this point,' he drawled when he'd finished. 'I don't want to offend your sensibilities.'

'You wouldn't!' she threw back, hoping to convince herself of it.

'No, perhaps not,' he surprised her by agreeing before he ran on, 'I forgot how experienced you are.'

'I meant you wouldn't dare!' she retorted.

'Well, that's where you're wrong, Kelly Cormack,' countered Ryan, deciding it was time the idiot girl learned when to back off.

Still treading water, Kelly watched in disbelief as he actually unzipped his trousers to strip down to undershorts and, without any further warning, dived cleanly into the pool.

From that moment on, panic took over. She struck out wildly for the shallow end of the pool, nearest the villa, but had swum just a few yards when a hand touched her leg. Thinking he meant to pull her underwater with him, she viciously kicked backwards and hit the wall of his ribs. Then she kept swimming, with every stroke expecting to be dragged under, until her hand touched the far edge and she felt a surge of triumph.

It was short-lived, as she began hauling herself out of the water, only to have an arm come round her waist to pull her back down. Too late, she realised he must have been right behind her all the time. And that he must have wanted her to reach the shallow end where, with his feet planted firmly on the base of the pool, he could trap her so easily.

Kelly still struggled on principle. First she made another attempt to boost herself on to the tiled surround, but his arm just dragged her down again. So she tried using an elbow, half raising it to drive back as hard as she could into his stomach. Except, instead of slackening his hold, he hauled her even closer. Then, after a full minute of straining and wrestling against his grip, she finally accepted the inevitable.

'Had enough?' demanded Ryan, not trusting her sudden stillness.

Positively wheezing for breath, Kelly could only answer with a nod. But it was taken as some form of submission, and the arm crushing her ribs immediately eased its pressure. When he pulled her round to face him, she hugged her breasts, trying to shield them from view. At the same time, she backed as far as she could against the side of the pool.

'You're a stubborn little fool, you know that?' Ryan said in a tone that was more exasperated than angry. 'And too damn provocative for your own good.'

'I didn't start this,' Kelly found the breath to protest.

His mouth went into a tight line. 'That's debatable, and in the present circumstances, I'd say highly irrelevant. It's how it finishes you should be worrying about.'

'What do you mean?' she scowled back.

Ryan couldn't believe she was that naïve. 'What do you think I mean?' He let his eyes drop to the naked swell of her breasts, not hidden by her crossed arms.

'Stop looking at me like that!' Kelly flushed, both angry and embarrassed, yet sure he was simply trying to scare her again.

'Be grateful I'm just looking,' he returned, eyes switching back to hers.

'If you lay a finger on me, I'll . . . I'll . . .' She searched desperately for a suitable threat.

'You'll . . .?' A mocking brow was raised.

'Oh, go to hell!' Kelly muttered in frustration and started to turn away.

It sparked off Ryan's temper once more, and he spun her round with such force that she fell against him. He put a hand to her waist, initially to steady her. But when she gave him a violent push, as if he really was attacking her, something inside him snapped.

Kelly found herself hauled against his chest, his arm trapping both of hers as he lifted her clear off the ground. Half in temper, half in fright, she screamed at him, 'Put me down, you bastard!'

But the hard glitter in his eyes should have told her he was beyond words, beyond control. Cruelly, a hand was thrust into her wet hair, dragging her head back, and a cry of indignation became pain as his mouth covered hers.

There was no desire in the kiss; forcing her lips back against her clenched teeth, it sought to dominate and humiliate. To teach Kelly how powerless she was, how vulnerable.

It was a hard lesson, and one she learned too late. Tears filled her eyes as she tried, in vain, to twist from his arms. Yet she kept trying, over and over, till strength and pride finally gave way in an anguished sob.

Eventually Ryan realised she was no longer fighting, and he broke off the kiss. At the sight of her frightened face, the fury that had driven him began to fade. Slowly he unfurled his fingers from her hair, his hand briefly touching her cheek as it fell away.

Kelly watched him with eyes as wary as a cornered animal's. He was looking at her so strangely. Almost puzzled, as if he'd forgotten who she was. Or perhaps he just wanted to, his eyes closing for a second.

Her hopes rose, taking it as a sign he would release her. But she couldn't have been more wrong, couldn't have been further from understanding what was going on in Ryan's head as he bent to kiss her again.

Only this time it was all so different, it might have been another man kissing her. Other hands caressing the nape of her neck, the curve of her spine. Other lips moving against hers, warm and persuasive.

At first Kelly was too stunned to react. She'd never been kissed like this before. No one had ever been allowed close enough.

But it seemed she could no more control Ryan Devlin than order her feelings. They were in total chaos, her mind knowing she hated this man, yet her body betraying her at his every touch. When he drew her to him, her soft breasts swelled against his harder flesh, her senses so confused she began to forget who he was, too. And, instead of pushing at his shoulders, her hands gradually reached round his neck, while her lips parted to answer the warm arousal of his.

Ryan gave a groan of pleasure, and for a moment Kelly felt as if the power was hers. Just for a moment, before the kiss became a total invasion—a passionate searching invasion that she wasn't ready for at all. Only, when she tried to draw back, his fingers threaded in her hair once more while the arm at her back slid downwards, lifting her body to his with a rough sensuality. And in that hungry, demanding kiss, power slipped away from her as shock went beyond fear to an unfamiliar emotion, trembling through her limbs like fever, whimpering in her throat like pain.

Then suddenly the hands at her waist were lifting her, up and out of the water, until she was sitting at the edge of the pool, staring at him in a daze.

'Go up to the house.' His instruction was so quiet she almost missed it. But, when she failed to move, it was followed by a harshly rapped, 'For God's sake, girl, get out of my sight!'

This time the disgust and loathing in his voice penetrated. Kelly didn't need another telling, she scrambled to her feet with a strangled cry. Wildly, blindly, she flew towards the villa—not looking back, running, tripping, falling a couple of steps as she raced up the back stairs to her room.

A child again, she threw herself face-down on the bed and, hands clutching at a pillow, let the tears fall. Tears of hurt at first, then of humiliation, gradually choking off to dry sobs until she rolled over on her back and asked herself why she was crying at all.

She had done nothing wrong. She'd fought him . . . at least in the beginning. And later? She tried to tell herself that she'd had no choice other than to submit. But she couldn't block out the memory of how she'd more than submitted, how she'd mindlessly responded to a kiss from a man who had given her every reason to dislike him.

A man she *did* dislike, Kelly decided fiercely, as her mind conjured up an image of his harshly handsome face. Only it scarcely made her response more acceptable—that she didn't even like the man, far less love him. In fact, it scared her.

For how different was she from her mother now? Her carelessly promiscuous mother. Not so different, perhaps. Maybe not different at all!

The thought was too disturbing to dwell on. She should forget the whole incident. Just pretend it had never happened. Assuming he had already gone, she didn't have to meet Ryan Devlin ever again. Tomorrow she would fly to Paris for a few days, then on to Egypt with Jay on the Friday.

That resolved, she rose from the bed and, putting on a T-shirt dress, went through to the adjoining bathroom. There she soaked her face in cold water to remove all trace of those rare tears.

It was when she returned to the bedroom that she heard voices drifting up from the terrace below. Padding cautiously to the balcony outside her window, she looked down and scowled at the sight of Ryan Devlin. He, too, had dressed and was now standing with Jay on the patio, deep in discussion.

Kelly caught her name once or twice, but little of what was being said. She watched the Australian shake his head at something, and didn't have time to draw back when he glanced towards the upper storey of the villa. Their eyes met for a second or two, his cold and unreadable, hers sullen and hostile. Then she turned away, ignoring Jay's call, and walked back to her bedroom.

Half an hour later there was a quiet knock on her door. 'It's Jay. May I come in, Kelly?'

'Yes...OK,' she agreed reluctantly.

Jay opened the door, saying, 'Listen, love, I——' but broke off mid-sentence when he spotted the almost packed suitcase on her bed.

'I thought I'd go to Paris a couple of days early. You don't mind, do you?' she asked as he crossed to her side.

'No, not as such...' he frowned uncertainly '...but what about Devlin?'

Kelly almost repeated a sarcastic 'what about Devlin?', sensing that in some way the Australian had brought Jay over to his side.

She confined herself to a mutter of, 'Has he gone?'

'Yes.'

'Good.'

'Kelly?' He caught her arm when she would have walked away. 'What happened between the two of you?'

Kelly heard the anxiety in his voice and realised how silly her earlier thoughts had been. The one person on whose support she could always rely was Jay. She just had to tell him that the younger man had forced himself on her, and there would be no question of whose side he'd take. But she found she couldn't bring herself to do it.

'What did *he* say happened?'

'Not much. Merely that you'd ended up quarrelling.'

'Well, that was about it.' Kelly tried to dismiss the subject with a shrug and went back to folding one of her shirts.

But Jay seemed determined to pursue it. 'He also said to tell you he was sorry.'

'He did?' Her eyes switched to him in disbelief.

'His exact words,' Jay nodded.

Kelly remained incredulous. 'Muttered through clenched teeth, I bet.'

'A trifle forced, possibly,' Jay conceded, smiling slightly at her astuteness. 'I assume you know *why* he was apologising.'

'For his existence, hopefully,' she replied, her tone unusually hard.

'That must have been some quarrel,' Jay sighed, then asked her, 'Did he explain *anything* to you beforehand? About why he was here, I mean?'

Kelly shook her head. 'What's going on, Jay?' She had a premonition that, whatever it was, she wasn't going to like it.

The premonition grew stronger as Jay put an arm round her shoulder. 'It's a long story, love. Why don't we go downstairs and I'll fix us both a drink, mm?'

'All right.' Kelly frowned in agreement and did not press for any further explanation as she followed him down the staircase to the lounge.

Jay didn't volunteer one either; instead, he relayed the latest production problems on his film.

Kelly made sympathetic noises in the right places, but remained on edge. For, over the last few months, Jay had broken other news in the same evasive fashion. Mostly it had concerned the chaotic state of her mother's finances.

Rarely out of work, Rhea Cormack had always spent liberally, loaning money to friends, borrowing on future earnings. By selling off assets, the debts had been met, but the chance of any of the loans being repaid was negligible; all that might be salvaged was a small percentage share of any profits from *Sunset Gold*. Kelly had accepted the situation philosophically.

Now she wondered if Ryan Devlin wasn't simply another debt collector. How her mother could come to owe money to some Australian defeated her, but perhaps that was Jay's long story.

He'd run out of casual conversation by the time he'd mixed their drinks and come to sit beside her on the sofa. She pulled a face at the strong smell of spirit in her gin and orange.

'That bad, is it?'

'Oh, no... At least, not necessarily... It depends...' So seldom at a loss for words, Jay was clearly struggling.

'Why don't you tell me straight out? It'll probably make it easier on both of us,' Kelly suggested with a smile.

Jay did not return it but, taking a deep breath, he quietly announced, 'Armand Duval wasn't your father, Kelly.'

A simple statement, it dropped like a softly exploding bombshell. At first, Kelly didn't feel a thing. No surprise, no pain, nothing. And, even when the shock-wave finally hit her, its effect was less devastating than might have been expected.

Had she known deep down? Not as a certainty, but hadn't there been pointers? Her mother had so rarely referred to Armand as 'your father', and had positively discouraged her when she'd once shown interest in meeting any French relatives she had. At the time, Kelly had thought it was because of her illegitimacy, but now she wondered. And what about some of the things her Irish grandmother had said during her final illness—had they just been delirium?

'You knew already?' Jay surmised from her almost calm reaction.

'I'm not sure,' she replied, her tone distracted. 'I mean, it makes sense of so many things, I feel I *should* have done. In fact, my grandmother as good as told me, only I ignored it. Perhaps I didn't want to know. Does that sound crazy?'

'No, of course not.' Her hand was taken and given a reassuring squeeze. 'I've shied away from confronting truths myself, at times. I'm afraid your mother did, too. But she did intend telling you some day.'

'Knowing Mother, she would probably have got round to it by my fortieth birthday,' Kelly commented, more in fond exasperation than bitterness.

'Probably,' Jay echoed drily before asking, 'What exactly *did* your grandmother say, Kelly?'

'Very little, really. Just how like my father I was— that I'd inherited his dark looks.'

'Which doesn't fit Armand.'

'Not as I recall, but at the time I convinced myself she was simply confused. I suppose I preferred to hang on to Armand,' Kelly reasoned, her lips twisting slightly. 'A case of better the father I knew than the one I didn't.'

'Would you still feel that way if I told you that he's alive and wants to see you?' Jay put in gently.

Kelly frowned as she realised who Ryan Devlin must be—an emissary from her father.

'I think so, yes,' she said after some consideration. 'Part of me is curious, naturally. But I suspect I can guess how the story goes. I mean, on Mother's form, he was more than likely a very nice man who had the bad luck to be both Catholic and married.'

Jay looked pained. 'I wish I could say you were wrong.'

'Oh, Jay, that wasn't intended as a dig against you! Honestly, it wasn't,' she stressed, lacing her fingers with his. 'If you were to turn round now and tell me *you* were my father, I'd be happy... more than happy.'

'If only I could,' he smiled sadly, and leaned forward to place a kiss on her forehead.

'Then let's pretend that's the way it is—not some stranger,' she suggested, seriousness behind the plea.

Jay had to shake his head. 'Not possible, my pet. Ryan Devlin's coming back tomorrow, and even if you left for Paris, I think he'd come after you. He wants to take you back to Australia, where your father lives.'

Kelly's expression changed to one of stubbornness. 'He can't force me to go anywhere.'

'No, of course not,' Jay agreed quickly. 'But it's what he might say that worries me. I think it would be better if you hear the truth from me, not him.'

'I suppose,' she nodded slowly, then remained silent as Jay began to recount the story Rhea Cormack had so long ago told him.

It was the story of a young girl from a small fishing village in Eire and the Irish Australian she had met at the county fair. A story of first-sight love, impulsive and beyond reason; forbidden love that had eventually taken them across to Paris where it could flourish and grow. Of stolen days, then weeks, months, with the promise that it would never end.

But, of course, it had. The Australian had put duty before love and returned to his cattle station, to the wife and family who needed him. The girl was left behind. Pregnant. An old, old story.

'Rhea wasn't bitter about it,' Jay added quietly. 'Though the man was older, she admitted that she had instigated the affair—or at least swept him along with her impulsiveness. She was also certain he would have stayed if he'd known about the baby.'

'She didn't tell him?'

'She only found out herself when he was back in Australia. By that time…well, she was beginning to face up to reality. Even if it had been possible, she couldn't see herself sharing his kind of life.'

Neither could Kelly, from what she imagined of Australian cattle stations. Her mother had enjoyed luxuries too much.

'It still must have been hard for her—coping alone in a strange city.'

'Oh, he didn't leave her penniless. In fact, he sent her both money and letters for months until finally she asked him to stop. After that, Armand helped her.'

'She knew him then, too?' Kelly said, visibly shocked.

'Only as a friend,' Jay was quick to stress. 'How they met, I'm not sure, but it was a good while after you were born when they started to live together.'

This assurance made Kelly feel slightly better, refuting the idea that her mother had simply passed from one man to another. 'My fath—Armand, he was even older, wasn't he?'

'About fifty, yes,' Jay confirmed. 'But that doesn't mean she didn't love him. To be honest, I think she loved him best of all,' he stated quietly.

Kelly could not deny it. Once, in a sad, reminiscent mood, her mother had said as much. At the time, she had taken it to be reassurance that she was at least a 'love child' in the truest of senses. Now, though she would have liked to keep believing that, she wasn't so certain any more.

'When did he find out about me—this Australian?'

'Not until you were six. He was over in Europe again. Rhea and he had long since lost touch, but apparently they ran into each other, quite by chance.' Jay recounted what he'd been told. 'You were with her, and it seems the likeness was too striking to miss. He wanted you then—or at least some part in your upbringing—but Rhea felt it would be confusing for you. So he agreed to wait until you were grown up.'

'I suppose he heard Mother was dead,' Kelly concluded.

'I imagine so,' Jay nodded. 'But as I say, his interest is neither sudden nor casual, Kelly. If he's held back till now, it's because he felt obliged to. And maybe I've been remiss in not telling you all this before.'

'You think I should go and see him, don't you?' she asked, frowning.

Jay paused. 'I think you should consider it, yes,' he said eventually.

Kelly, however, had much bigger reservations. 'I don't know, Jay. Even accepting I might want to see him, surely I'd be an embarrassment to his family?'

'If you're thinking of his wife, she's been dead some years. And as far as I know, there's only the one son.'

'But *he* must object,' she insisted.

'Well, possibly you have got off on the wrong foot,' Jay said with a slight smile, 'but I doubt he'd have come all this way looking for you, if he objected.'

'You mean . . . you can't mean . . .' Kelly refused to believe she'd understood.

Obliquely, Jay confirmed her fears by murmuring, 'I thought you'd realised.' Then, registering she was shocked—far more shocked—at gaining a half-brother than a new father, he asked, 'What *did* happen between you and Devlin, Kelly?'

But Kelly scarcely heard him, for her mind was screaming, *He can't be! He can't be!* Over and over the words were repeated as her mind flicked through images and, like a voyeur, sickly fascinated, watched herself in Ryan Devlin's arms, her body lifting from the pool, curving to his, surrendering . . .

'Kelly?' Jay pressed her arm.

She stared at him sightlessly and, though her lips moved, no sound came out.

'Here, drink this!' He picked up her untouched drink and, getting little response, tilted the glass so she was forced to swallow.

More gin than orange, the spirit had the desired effect as it burned the back of her throat and she started coughing.

'OK?' Jay patted her back and she nodded, her eyes losing their glazed expression. But, when he repeated his earlier question, they became guarded, then slid away altogether.

'Nothing happened, I told you.' Slow to come, the lie rang hollow.

'Something must have, love,' Jay insisted. 'You went positively white when you discovered Devlin was your brother.'

'He isn't!' This time her reply was immediate.

Jay misunderstood, and amended, humouring her, 'All right, your half-brother.'

Kelly bit back another denial. If she kept protesting, Jay would expect a reason. And she didn't have one—didn't have a rational reason beyond her instinctive, horrified refusal to accept the situation.

She pictured Ryan Devlin's face, first when he'd closed his eyes to shut out the sight of her, then later when he'd lifted her from the pool. She heard again the disgust in his voice, rapping out the order to get up to the house. And finally it struck her how both near and far she had been from understanding.

In temper, he had forgotten who she was, and in remembering, *knowing*, he too had been horrified.

'Did he insult your mother—is that it?' Jay suggested at her lengthening silence.

'Yes . . . yes, he insulted my mother,' she seized the excuse, repeating it almost word for word.

Jay didn't seem to notice, running on, 'Well, maybe that isn't so unnatural, love—not if he holds Rhea responsible for hurting his parents' marriage.'

But Kelly was in no mood to appreciate his peace-making talents, and she rose from the sofa.

'Where are you going?' he asked, alarmed by the sudden move.

'Just to my room, if you don't mind.'

'No...no, of course not. This must have all come as a shock to you. I imagine you need time to think it over.'

Kelly gave a small nod, as if agreeing. But it was more to reassure Jay. For she didn't need time. She knew it was impossible to meet her father without seeing Ryan Devlin again. And that she wasn't prepared to do.

She went up to her room and once more lay on the bed. But this time she didn't cry. She was beyond tears, locked in some dark corner of her mind.

She shut her eyes, and still the images came: of two bodies straining together, of a dark head raised to a fair one, of a kiss that should never have been. And still she remembered how it had felt, that dizzy confusion of pleasure and desire.

Even the later shock had not wiped out the memory. It scared her too much. It scared her that she could be so open, so vulnerable. Perhaps she really had inherited her mother's weakness and her 'talent' for picking the wrong man.

Wrong? What an understatement that was! How much more wrong could it have been? She and Devlin, with nothing in common—nothing except for the blood which ran in their veins.

And that fact left Kelly feeling sick with shame.

CHAPTER FOUR

KELLY passed a restless night, and woke the next morning, still as determined to avoid any further contact with the man who had so carelessly turned her world upside-down.

Fortunately Jay had gone back to keeping more regular hours, and over breakfast she stated her intentions. At first he tried to persuade her into taking a more reasonable approach, but eventually it got through to him that Kelly had absolutely no wish to be reasonable. She stood staring out of the french windows for almost two hours until the white BMW appeared at the villa gates. Then she retreated to her bedroom, leaving him to act as messenger.

Quarter of an hour later, however, he came upstairs to relay with a sigh, 'I'm sorry, Kelly, he's insisting on talking to you personally.'

'Didn't you tell him?' she appealed, her brows knitting in a frown.

Jay crossed to stand beside her chair. 'Oh, yes, I made it quite plain you have no intention of going to Australia, but...' He gave a helpless shrug to convey how little impression it had had on the younger man.

'I don't want to see him, Jay.'

'Yes, I know.' He laid a reassuring hand on her shoulder. 'And I won't force you. The only trouble is, I'm not certain how to get rid of him.'

'You could throw him out,' Kelly suggested, without considering practicalities.

Jay already had, correcting wryly, 'I could try. I doubt I'd succeed.'

'No.' Kelly pulled a face, remembering all too well Ryan Devlin's muscular strength. 'We could call the local *gendarmerie*,' she proposed as an alternative.

'You can't be serious!'

'Why not?' Kelly positively favoured the idea of the Australian being thrown into a French gaol.

'Well, for one thing, you can picture the headlines if the story ever got out.'

'You think Devlin would tell the Press?'

'Not deliberately, no,' Jay shook his head. 'But if we have him arrested, he's bound to explain his side to the police, and it could leak from there.'

'Yes, I suppose so,' Kelly agreed reluctantly. 'What else can we do?'

Jay spread his hands in a gesture of defeat. 'Short of staying here and hoping he just goes away, I don't know.'

'But Dale's coming to pick you up soon,' she frowned, reminding him of the lunch date he had with the producer and one of the backers of their next film.

'Perhaps I should phone and cancel,' he suggested.

'No, that would be silly.' Kelly began to feel it wrong to expect Jay to fight her battles and, reluctantly accepting the inevitable, rose to her feet. 'OK, let's get it over with.'

'You're going down?' Her tight-lipped nod left a surprised Jay unsure whether to be more relieved or worried.

The Australian was by the french windows, looking out on to the courtyard, and he turned at the sound of their tread on the hardwood stairs. His eyes immediately sought Kelly's.

To Jay, it seemed as if an unspoken apology was being transmitted. But, glancing at Kelly, he saw no sign that it was recognised as such. Her gaze was remote, her manner haughty when she finally spoke. 'You wished to talk to me about something, Mr Devlin?'

Jay suppressed a groan as he waited for the Australian's response.

It was brief, equally stiff-necked. 'Privately, yes.'

'I have no secrets from Mr Rutherford,' Kelly claimed rather rashly.

In contrast, Ryan's reply was measured—quiet and purposeful. *'Haven't you?'*

He didn't add to it. He didn't need to. This time the look they exchanged was one of perfect understanding.

Puzzled, Jay's eyes switched between the two. 'What does he mean, Kelly?'

'Nothing,' she dismissed with a guilty flush.

Ryan Devlin showed more composure, admitting, 'I'm afraid I said some things in temper yesterday that I'd find easier to apologise for without an audience.'

If not wholly convinced, Jay was swayed by the possibility of a reconciliation. 'Kelly?' He lifted an enquiring brow in her direction.

Kelly didn't see she had much choice. 'Well, if Mr Devlin feels the need to apologise...' she said with deadpan sarcasm.

If Mr Devlin did, he awarded her a distinctly unapologetic look.

She collected a gently reproving frown from Jay, too, before he suggested, 'Why don't you take Mr Devlin out to the patio while I brew some coffee?'

Wordlessly, Kelly obeyed the prompt, leading the way to the table and chairs on the back terrace. And just as wordlessly she sat down to concentrate all her attention on the cracks in the patio flagstone.

Ryan took the chair opposite and waited patiently for her to acknowledge his presence. He'd promised himself that this time he wasn't going to lose his temper.

But, after a minute stretched to two, he realised his patient approach might have them still sitting there at sunset.

'Look, I accept you have the right to be annoyed,' he finally announced.

'Annoyed?' The colossal understatement had Kelly forgetting any resolve to ignore him. 'Is that it? Your

apology? You accept I have the right to be annoyed,'
she taunted, with a fair mimicry of his Australian drawl.

Ryan took a deep breath, counted slowly to ten, then
managed a restrained, 'Not all of it, no.'

'Well, if that's an example, I'd skip the rest,' she advised flippantly.

'OK! Fine by me!' he almost barked back. 'But let's
get one thing straight, with regards to our relationship——'

'As far as I'm concerned, we don't have one,' she cut
in rudely.

'My point exactly,' he agreed on a meaningful note.

But Kelly misunderstood as she scowled, 'Then, if you
feel the same way, why did you bother to come looking
for me?'

'Right at this moment, I can't think of a single good
reason,' Ryan muttered, his gaze resting on the impudent curve of her mouth. 'Other than possibly some
obligation to your father.'

'*Your* father, not mine!' Kelly retorted, feeling bloody-
minded.

'Try switching that round and you'll have the right
idea,' he suggested shortly.

It made Kelly pause for a moment before demanding,
'What's that supposed to mean?'

'If you shut up long enough, I just might tell you.'
Ryan sent her a quelling glance, and only when her lips
had formed a sullen, compressed line did he continue
soberly, 'Whether you want to accept it or not, there
can be no doubt Paddy Devlin's your father. Looks alone
substantiate the fact. However, he *isn't* mine. At least,
not in the natural sense... I was adopted,' he finished
on an abrupt note.

Though Kelly's eyes had widened in surprise, she didn't
question that he was telling the truth. *This*, she wanted
to believe. It sent a great wave of relief through her that
her first reaction had been so instinctively right—he
couldn't be her brother.

But then relief gradually gave way to anger as she recalled the doubts and the shame she'd later felt. She glared at him accusingly. 'Why didn't you say anything?'

'I've been trying to for the last ten minutes,' he drily pointed out.

'Yesterday, I mean!' she snapped.

'Yesterday?' He gave her an incredulous look. 'And when do you imagine I had the opportunity to do that? In the five seconds it took for you to start another argument? Or maybe after you dived into the pool and started throwing childish taunts at me?' he suggested in mocking tones. 'And always assuming you'd allowed me a chance, what should I have said? That, apart from not being a reporter, I wasn't your brother either? That would have made a hell of a lot of sense to you then, would it?'

Kelly saw his point—just. But it didn't account for his earlier silence.

'Why didn't you tell me who you were the first day?' she asked suspiciously.

'Because you obviously didn't know me from Adam,' he replied, 'and I thought it might be better to leave you in ignorance.'

Kelly frowned as she wished he had.

'Look, I know I handled things badly,' Ryan went on to admit. 'I'm also sorry about yesterday when I...well, when I lost my temper. However, you can be quite certain nothing like that will happen again,' he assured stiffly.

Why he felt the need to escaped Kelly. It was unlikely they'd ever meet after today.

'What I'm saying is,' he continued at her lack of response, 'you have no reason to fear I'd...I'd make any further advances towards you.'

'I didn't imagine you would,' Kelly put in before he could become any more explicit.

'Well, as long as you understand,' he muttered with an awkwardness that made her wonder if she was the only one being embarrassed by this conversation.

Certainly, they both looked relieved when Jay appeared to place a tray of coffee on the table.

He did not sit down but, smiling slightly, enquired, 'Everything sorted out?'

'Not quite,' Ryan replied, then staggered Kelly by adding, 'We were just discussing Kelly's returning to Australia.'

It was such an outrageous lie, she didn't even attempt to counter it. But if she thought Jay couldn't possibly be taken in, there was only surprise in his, 'You've changed your mind?'

This time she managed to open her mouth before Ryan cut in, 'She's considering it, yes.'

And Jay responded with gentle irony, 'Progress, indeed. You must have a way with words, Mr Devlin.'

A twisting way, Kelly nearly said, but confined herself to muttering, 'Nothing's decided yet,' a stubborn note in her voice.

It had Jay turning to quietly reassure her with, 'Well, no one is going to rush you, Kelly. You know that whatever you choose to do will be fine by me.'

Not by Ryan Devlin, though. Kelly recognised that from the contempt in his watching eyes as Jay gently squeezed her shoulder. Again, however, she kept her thoughts to herself. Time enough to convey her real feelings when the Australian left.

But she'd forgotten Jay's lunch appointment. The prolonged blast of a horn from the front courtyard came as an abrupt reminder.

'That'll be Dale, telling me we're already late,' he explained, then sent her a quizzical glance.

From it, Kelly knew that if she asked he would stay. So it was an act of unselfishness for her to reply, 'You'd better hurry.'

An act she began to regret the moment he'd departed with a quick kiss on her cheek.

'I must admit I have yet to figure out your *friend*, Rutherford,' the Australian remarked almost conversationally.

But she still bristled, 'In what respect, precisely?'

'Oh, don't get me wrong,' he added. 'On balance, he seems a decent man. The thing that puzzles me is his willingness to let you go.'

Kelly shrugged, not seeing anything very puzzling about it, and pointed out, 'It's *my* willingness which counts.'

'To a degree,' he conceded.

'Totally,' she countered.

Grey eyes narrowed on her. 'I take it that means you're against the idea at present.'

'Totally,' she repeated, 'and I wouldn't hold your breath, either.'

Ryan found it was his temper he had to hold. 'Would you like to explain why you're not prepared to go?'

'Right at the moment I can't think of a single good reason *to* go,' Kelly stated, deadly serious behind the flippancy.

'Then I'll give you one,' Ryan rapped back. 'Against my better judgement, I've travelled thousands of miles searching for you—and all because a sentimental old man wants to offer a home to a daughter he scarcely knows. He's waited fourteen years for your selfish mother to grant him that *privilege*, and he may not have another fourteen to wait until the fancy takes you to pay him a visit. Just think on that!' he finished angrily.

Kelly had thought on it, had considered the feelings that prompted her father to send for her. But they didn't outweigh her dislike for the younger Devlin.

'I don't need a home,' she eventually said. 'And if that's all he's concerned about, you can tell him I'm OK.'

'It isn't,' he denied shortly. 'I've already telegraphed, informing him of your situation.'

Kelly frowned. 'By situation, I assume you mean my staying with Jay.'

'I told him you were living with an older man, yes,' he confirmed, but changing the whole emphasis.

'You don't think——' Kelly broke off, questioning if she could possibly have understood him. Surely he didn't imagine that she and Jay—that they were... No, it was too ridiculous.

But then he ran on, 'I don't think anything. As far as I'm concerned, your relationship with Rutherford is your own business.'

'My *relationship* with Jay,' Kelly grated back, 'consists of my keeping house for him while he, in return, keeps me. That is until such time as I can afford to do so myself. I trust I've made myself clear.'

She hadn't totally, as Ryan was left wondering if she was denying having an affair with the older man or justifying it. Either way, he didn't trust her word for anything.

'I would have thought you could afford just about anything. After all, your mother must have earned a fortune in her lifetime.'

'She also spent a fortune.'

'On what?' he asked at this dry admission.

'Enjoying life,' she shrugged in reply.

And Ryan concluded, 'You must resent her for leaving you penniless.'

'Must I? Why?'

'Just that some people might think it pretty careless she didn't make provision for your future.'

'Then *some people* would be wrong,' Kelly retorted. 'And if you measure caring in monetary terms, Mr Devlin, that doesn't say a whole lot for the relationships in *your* life.'

Temper roused, she didn't stop to consider her words, but they obviously hit a nerve as his jaw clenched and his eyes became the coldest grey she had ever seen.

He responded in an intimidatingly low voice, 'Whereas you, Miss Cormack, have already said too much.'

And for a moment Kelly was intimidated, or at least sensitive to some dark, suppressed emotion behind his coldness. It put her on the defensive. 'Well, you started it—jumping to conclusions about me and Jay. And, worse, broadcasting them all over the place.'

'Only to my... to Paddy. I felt he should know your *circumstances*.' His lips twisted on the word before he slipped a hand into his jacket and withdrew a piece of paper. 'Not that it made the smallest impression. Here, this is his reply. It should give you some idea of his feelings.'

Kelly picked up the telegram that had been tossed on the table in front of her and, smoothing it out, read:

DON'T SIT IN JUDGEMENT, SON. JUST
BRING HER HOME. PLEASE.
PADDY

Though brief, its tone did convey something of the writer. Not an unpleasant image either, despite the note of criticism. Or perhaps because of it, Kelly was honest enough to admit.

'Is he like how he sounds?' she asked, her first positive interest.

'That depends—how does he sound to you?'

She re-read the brief telegram, but in the end shook her head, deciding it was silly to try and form an opinion on a couple of phrases.

'Most people find him very easy-going,' Ryan volunteered. 'You'll be able to judge for yourself when you come over.'

Kelly picked up the 'when' and raised her eyes from the telegram. 'I haven't changed my mind yet.'

Tactically, Ryan decided not to argue the point. Instead he held up his hands in a gesture of truce. Then he nodded towards the tray brought out by Rutherford, so far untouched.

'Do you think I might have a cup of coffee?'

'Yes, of course.'

Taking it as a reproof to her manners, Kelly snatched up the coffee jug and, after pouring two cups, went through the ritual of asking whether he took milk or sugar—polite formalities that sounded totally absurd in the circumstances.

Then silence reigned as the coffee was drunk, a silence that stretched while Kelly again wondered what her father was like, and asked herself if Ryan had been right in part: that, despite her adamant refusal, one day something would prompt her to go to Australia. Perhaps to find out if she bore more than a physical resemblance to the man who had fathered her.

Finally she broke the silence with an impulsive, 'You're wrong about Jay and me, you know. And I want you to tell him that.'

Ryan, who had been studying her downturned face, was quick to shield his satisfaction. He took the words as a sign her stance was changing.

'If you like,' he agreed.

She wasn't fooled. 'You still don't believe me, do you?'

'Is my opinion important to you?' he shrugged.

'Not in the least,' pride had Kelly throwing back.

'Well, I shouldn't worry about Paddy,' he continued drily. 'He'll probably believe anything you care to tell him.'

'Less of a cynic, is he?' she retorted.

'In your case, definitely. But then he still remembers you as a pretty little girl, with a head of dark curls and a winning smile,' he said in a tone that had to be sarcastic.

She awarded him a glower. 'I suppose you're referring to the time we met . . . in Paris.'

'Yes, only it was in Dublin, not Paris. In the lobby of the Shelbourne Hotel, to be exact.'

'Jay seemed to think it was an accident.'

'True enough—a pure coincidence. You were there for a family wedding, while we were celebrating my coming of age with a trip to the "old country".'

Up to then, Kelly hadn't realised *he* had been present. Curious, she asked, 'What happened?'

'Oh, your mother did her best to carry off the situation, pretending they were casual acquaintances,' he relayed with a humourless laugh. 'But Paddy doesn't have her acting abilities. He just stood there, dumbly staring at you.'

'He guessed who I was?'

'Almost instantly, I would think. Though you were only about six, the likeness was already very marked.' Cold, grey eyes once more assessed her distinctive features. 'If I hadn't been distracted by your mother, it might have struck me, too.'

'So you didn't realise?'

'Not until your mother's lover, the Frenchman, appeared. You called him "Papa", I remember. Then no one could miss the stricken look on Paddy's face.'

'It must have been a shock for you, too,' Kelly said on a genuinely sympathetic impulse.

It was instantly rejected as he clipped out, 'I survived.'

'Obviously!' she snapped in return, feeling foolish for imagining he might have been hurt by the incident. He'd probably been just as hard all those years ago—when she'd been six and he an already grown-up twenty-one.

'Anyway,' he went on curtly, 'your mother promised Paddy that later, when you were older, she'd send you to visit him.'

'And I'm sure *you* think she should have,' Kelly commented, eyes sceptical.

'It might have been a damn sight better for you if she had,' Ryan retaliated. 'Better, at any rate, than letting you run wild in Ireland.'

'What gives you the idea I did?' Kelly frowned.

'I was in County Clare two weeks ago,' he announced, as if it confirmed everything.

'Oh, *I* see. We've been talking to *dear* Aunt Mary,' she concluded, her tone changing to scorn. 'And what did she have to say—nothing good, I trust?'

'Absolutely nothing,' he agreed with crushing emphasis.

To little effect as Kelly retorted, 'Still predicting a dire end for me, was she?'

'That was the general refrain.' Ryan's lips went into an even grimmer line. 'Your finishing school's, too.'

'You have been busy, haven't you?' She looked at him with disdain.

'Your aunt didn't know your whereabouts, so I tried the school,' Ryan found himself justifying his actions. 'One of your old classmates suggested you might be at the Arbois.'

'And no doubt Madame Brunel herself told you about my expulsion,' Kelly surmised. 'In suitably lurid detail, too, I bet.'

'She told me you'd been caught sleeping with some ski instructor, yes,' he stated bluntly.

And naturally he'd believed it, Kelly saw from the contempt in his eyes. She could almost hear her ex-headmistress saying the words: free and easy, just like her mother.

'You're not going to deny it?' he challenged at her silence.

'You'll think what you want anyway.' Kelly didn't intend wasting breath explaining herself. Instead, she tilted her head back, a gesture of defiance rather than the shame he might have expected.

'Doesn't it bother you at all—the way people are talking about you?' he demanded.

'As you're the only one doing the talking—no, it doesn't,' she said, returning his derisive stare.

'Don't kid yourself!' he laughed, short and harsh. 'Do you want to know how I finally found you? I overheard a couple of women discussing how like your mother you are—and they *weren't* referring to your appearance.'

This knocked some of the confidence out of Kelly, though she muttered, 'If you mean Stella Martin, everybody knows she makes up gossip as she goes along.'

'Perhaps she does. But she didn't make up your living with Rutherford, and she won't be alone in thinking you're simply using him.'

'Using him ... how?'

'To get into pictures the easy way,' the Australian explained at her puzzled look.

And Kelly flared back, 'That's rubbish! Utter rubbish! For a start, I don't even *want* a film career. What's more, nobody else sees my friendship with Jay like that.'

'Don't they?' Ryan played on her obvious uncertainty.

'No!' she denied crossly, and almost knocked back her chair as she stood up.

He rose quickly to block her path. 'Don't think you're running out on me this time!'

'I'm not!' Kelly snapped back. 'If you must know, I'm just going to telephone someone. All right?' she requested in a purely sarcastic vein and, not waiting for a response, brushed past him to stalk off inside.

She went through the lounge to the far kitchen and the telephone extension there. Then she took a calming breath before dialling the Arbois and asking for Suzie Bryant.

'Hi. Are you coming down this afternoon?' her friend said by way of greeting.

'I'm not sure. Listen, is your mother around?' she enquired cautiously.

Suzie matched her lowered tone, 'No, she's gone shopping. Why?'

'I wanted to ask you something,' Kelly said hesitantly.

'Shoot!' invited Suzie.

So she plunged on, 'OK. Have you heard any rumours about myself and Jay?'

'Rumours?' Suzie echoed, then paused before saying, 'What sort of rumours?'

'As in my supposedly having an affair with him,' Kelly added bluntly.

'Oh,' came back in a telling murmur.

'Please, Suz, the truth?' she appealed.

And her friend burst out, 'But it's just too absurd! I mean, everybody knows it is, Kelly. I didn't believe it for a single second, and neither did Simon. In fact, he went flip when someone implied that you and Jay were...well, it's absurd...' Suzie trailed off as she realised her attempts at reassurance were missing their mark by a mile.

From them, Kelly deduced the rumour was on general release. How naïve she'd been! She had never even considered her living with Jay might be misunderstood.

'Kelly, are you still there?'

'Yes.'

'Look, I would have told you before, but——'

'It's OK, Suz, I understand,' Kelly put in quietly.

'Well...if I were you, I'd just forget it,' Suzie said after another awkward pause.

'I suppose so,' Kelly murmured in agreement, then with a last, 'See you,' rang off.

But she already knew it wasn't going to be so simple. It was one matter to shrug off Ryan Devlin's opinion, quite another to ignore gossip on a much wider scale. With scandalmongers like Stella Martin about, it surely wouldn't be long before the trashier magazines picked up the story. And there was little doubt what interpretation *they* would put on her living with Jay!

Kelly's heart sank at the idea. She just couldn't face being hounded by them all over again. It had been bad enough after the car crash, when they'd besieged the house for weeks, until Kelly had been almost glad to hand it over to her mother's creditors. She'd come to Europe to escape the publicity, and had avoided the awards ceremony at Cannes for the same reason. But, if this story leaked out, they'd actively track her down.

And it wouldn't just be her name they'd drag through the gutter. She was nobody compared with Jay. He'd be the main feature, his life put under their dirty little microscopes. Whatever else happened, she had to prevent that. The question was how.

Minutes ticked by as she sat slumped at the kitchen table, head in hands, desperately searching for a way out and, unhappily, finding only one.

Eventually it came looking for her, obviously impatient at her prolonged absence.

Kelly said without preamble, 'When do we leave?'

'For Australia?' Her sudden capitulation caught Ryan unprepared.

'Unless you've changed your mind.' Kelly shrugged as if it didn't matter to her either way.

Ryan shook his head. 'May I ask why you've changed yours?'

He could ask, but she wasn't about to tell him. Pride wouldn't allow her to admit that she was running away—and had simply nowhere else to go.

'Perhaps the fancy has just taken me,' she suggested flippantly.

Only to be warned, 'It's not going to be some pleasure trip, you know.'

'No, I don't imagine for one moment that it will be,' Kelly returned with heavy irony.

It left Ryan wondering why he still felt like shaking her, even when she ended up agreeing with him.

CHAPTER FIVE

'FASTEN your seat-belts, please,' the Australian stewardess echoed, as the instruction flashed on an overhead sign.

Kelly responded automatically. In the last week she'd heard the same words repeated with monotonous regularity. And though they were finally arriving at a small airport outside the town of Katherine, Northern Territory, she was too tired to care. For, far from pleasurable, the trip had turned out to be a gruelling marathon of plane journeys, taxi rides and tedious delays.

First they'd flown from Nice to London where two days were spent haunting Australia House, queuing and form-filling until a short-term visa was obtained for Kelly. It had been a tiresome process, fraying tempers on several occasions. By the time they boarded an eastbound Qantas jet, their conversation had been reduced to bare necessities.

Twenty strained hours later, they arrived in Singapore for a stopover. Kelly was too jet-lagged to appreciate what some regard as one of the most interesting cities in the world. She dozed off in the taxi ride from the airport and, still drowsy, was guided up the hotel steps by Ryan, a light hand on her back.

She was also giving a fair imitation of falling asleep in the lift, when it jolted to a rather abrupt halt. She swayed on her feet and suddenly found herself being picked up bodily by a pair of strong arms.

For a moment the breath was knocked from her, then she almost squealed in protest, 'What are you doing?'

'Sweeping you off your feet—what do you think?' Ryan answered drily.

Kelly flushed at the sarcasm, and concentrated on staring rigidly over his shoulder. In doing so, she caught their two Chinese porters exchanging grins as they trailed behind with the baggage. Evidently they'd put their own interpretation on this Western behaviour and, after depositing Kelly's cases in the first bedroom, they discreetly withdrew to wait for Ryan in the corridor.

Meanwhile, Kelly couldn't wait to get out of his arms. The instant they were alone, she said imperiously, 'You may put me down.'

'Oh, *may I*?' Ryan raised a brow at her tone and deliberately ignored the order.

Apart from seethe in frustration, there was little Kelly could do. While their eyes locked in a silent battle of wills, she became stiflingly conscious of his closeness, of the smell of his aftershave, of the muscular rise and fall of his chest, and the coolness of his breath against the warmth of her skin.

'Please let me down, Ryan,' she finally said with an odd, husky quality in her voice.

Plainly a surrender—she watched for the look of triumph to appear on his face. But it never came. His eyes just kept holding hers, even when he'd set her back on the ground.

In the end, she found his stare as disturbing as his closeness, and she asked nervously, 'Is something wrong?'

It distracted him, his gaze losing some of that strange intensity as he returned, 'Not wrong, no. I was just thinking how young you look—like a child, almost.'

'Well, I'm not!' Kelly stated crossly.

Yet she didn't feel any better when he agreed, 'No, I don't suppose you are any more. But maybe that's a pity. At least, it would have been easier.'

'Easier?' she echoed.

'To treat you the way Paddy expects me to.'

'And how is that, exactly?'

The question made him smile—a thin, humourless smile as he said, 'Like my little sister, of course.'

'I'm not *that*, either!' Kelly scowled back.

'Oh, don't worry—I have no brotherly feelings towards you whatsoever,' he assured with a mocking edge.

'I never imagined you had,' she retorted. 'In fact, you've made your dislike of me quite plain.'

'*Dislike*?' he echoed, this time giving an incredulous laugh. 'You really think it's that simple—what I feel for you?'

'All right, contempt, if you prefer.' Kelly assumed he was objecting to the mildness of the word 'dislike'.

But he shook his head. 'You don't understand, do you? It's not a question of contempt or dislike... I just wish you could have been someone else, that's all,' he concluded quietly, his eyes holding hers once more.

He was right, Kelly didn't understand. She stared back at him in silence, trying to read the thoughts behind those grave, grey eyes of his. But she was already too late: the shutters had come down, blanking off all emotion. He was gone from her even before he turned and walked out of the room.

Kelly stood frowning after him, still lost as to what he'd meant. How could he claim *not* to dislike her, yet most of the time act as if he did? It didn't make sense. It just left her feeling confused and more distrustful than ever.

In the morning she'd almost been relieved to find him back on his best bad-tempered form. He had begun the day by banging on her door to tell her she'd slept through their wake-up call. Then, at the airport, he'd let her know exactly whose fault it was that they'd missed their scheduled flight to Darwin.

Fortunately there were vacant seats on a later plane, which also connected with the afternoon flight to Katherine. But he was uncommunicative during the journey and hardly more talkative when they lunched in

Darwin. In fact, except for his enquiring what she wished to drink with the meal, Kelly might have been invisible.

She was reminded of her first image of him—as perfect casting for the 'strong, silent type'. Or had the image originally been Suzie's? Poor, susceptible Suzie, who'd gone into envious raptures over her disappearing into the sunset with the Australian.

Kelly wondered just how envious her friend would be if she could see her now, sitting with a stuffed dummy for company. She smiled wryly at the thought.

'What's the joke?' Ryan asked.

'Nothing,' Kelly replied, but felt her cheeks tinge a guilty pink. 'I was just wondering...um...what it's like in the Outback,' she added rather lamely.

At any rate, it drew a suspicious look before he answered, 'Hot, dry and dusty.'

'All the time?' she said doubtfully.

'No, in the summer it's humid instead of dry, and we get the occasional typhoon,' he continued, painting an even more inhospitable picture.

And Kelly muttered under her breath, 'Welcome to Australia,' thinking that, if all the inhabitants were like Ryan Devlin, they couldn't have much of a tourist industry.

After that, she lapsed into silence, deciding she'd see the place for herself, soon enough...

Only now, as her mind was brought back to the present by their final touchdown at Katherine airport, Kelly realised it was *too* soon. She looked out at the small group of terminal buildings, then back to a distant-faced Ryan at her side. And she suddenly knew, with absolute certainty, that she'd made the biggest mistake of her young life.

In truth, she'd begun suspecting it before they'd even reached London. He'd cold-shouldered her on that flight too, having already shown his impatience during her emotional farewell with Jay at Nice Airport. And, once in London, he'd spent much of the time snapping her head off.

So why hadn't she had the sense to call off the whole trip then, instead of letting some silly gossip drive her away from Jay, who liked and cared for her? Instead of letting panic carry her to the back end of nowhere with this man who took every opportunity to show how much he *disliked* her? Why hadn't she seen that the cure might prove worse than the disease?

All the guide-books had warned her she would either love or hate the wild, rugged country of the Outback and its tough, single-minded individuals. But it was only now that the idea that Ryan Devlin might be typical of the Outback male struck her with all its appalling possibilities. What if everybody on the cattle station treated her the way he did—as a mixture of oddity and idiot?

Kelly tried to dismiss such thoughts as the plane taxied to a halt, but they were to return full force later, when she walked through the arrival gates.

Ryan had told her they were to be met by the cattle station's head stockman and, on imagination alone, she could have picked him out from the waiting crowd. A tall, rangy figure dressed in khakis, with sun-creased eyes and an angular face burnt leather-brown, he might be darker-haired and less handsome than Ryan, but the similarity was there. While he bore down on them, a dispirited Kelly began fading into the background, wishing she could fade away altogether.

Evidently friends, the two men exchanged warm handshakes. The stockman had a voice which carried, and Kelly heard him joke that some little French *mademoiselle* was responsible for Ryan's extended holiday. A man-to-man comment, it suggested he had yet to notice her, hovering behind.

Perhaps if he had, he wouldn't have gone on to drawl, 'Sexiest women in the world, those French ladies.'

'So they say,' Ryan laughed, without rising to the bait.

Then he glanced round to locate Kelly, standing a few feet away, but plainly listening to every word. He looked at her as if she was a troublesome piece of baggage he'd wanted to forget.

She pulled a slight face in return, while the other Australian belatedly acknowledged her existence with an open-mouthed stare.

A bare introduction was supplied. 'Jeff, this is Kelly.'

'Er, how do you, miss...*mademoiselle*?' the stockman mumbled, seemingly having French women on the brain.

At any rate, a sense of mischief prompted Kelly to echo, *'Bien, merci. Et comment allez-vous, monsieur?'*

'I don't...um...' Shaking his head, the bewildered Australian gave up and consulted Ryan. 'What's she saying?'

'God knows,' he muttered, sending a threatening glare in her direction.

Undeterred, Kelly responded with a smile of pure insolence. But it changed to one of pleasantness when she addressed the other man, 'I'm sorry about the French. I only meant it as a joke.'

The apology was instantly accepted as he grinned back. 'That's OK. What was it you said?'

'Oh, just that I was well. And how are you?' she repeated with a questioning lift.

'Fine, thanks...*Kelly*, is it?' he said uncertainly.

She nodded. 'Same as the Irish surname. Sounds a bit funny, I suppose.'

'No, it's a pretty name. Suits you,' he added, his eyes now admiring Kelly in her bright yellow, cotton sundress. Then, obviously trying to place who she was, he asked, 'Are you out here on holiday?'

'In a way,' she replied briefly, leaving a fuller explanation to Ryan.

'Paddy didn't mention Kelly to you?' he queried and, when the other man shook his head, hesitantly supplied, 'She's a relative of ours.'

'Is that so?' Surprised, Jeff switched his eyes back to Kelly.

Kelly was surprised, too—at the phrase 'a relative of ours'. She threw Ryan a quizzical glance.

'You know,' Jeff continued, studying her face, 'now you've told me, I can see a pretty fair likeness to Paddy round the eyes and mouth. You must be quite a close relation—a niece or something.'

'Or something,' Kelly echoed, once more looking to Ryan.

This time he announced, 'Her mother and Paddy were first cousins.'

And, while Kelly positively gaped at him, Jeff swallowed the lie whole, concluding, 'Which makes you sort of second cousins, doesn't it?'

Ryan nodded, then quickly changed the subject. 'How did you come—by air or road?'

'Road, I'm afraid. The Cessna's out at one of the mustering camps, and the Nomad's crook again. Damn plane—Paddy thinks we should scrap it.'

'He's probably right,' Ryan frowned, disgruntled by the information.

'I've brought the best jeep, though,' Jeff directed reassuringly at a silent Kelly. 'I'll go drive it round to the front—save you a walk.'

Not trusting herself to respond civilly, Kelly didn't respond at all. But, the moment the other man was out of range, she exploded at Ryan, 'Why the hell did you tell him that rubbish?'

'Rubbish?' He had the nerve to look blank.

'About my mother and your fath—Paddy being cousins,' Kelly enlarged, quite unnecessarily, she was sure.

'I had to account for you somehow,' he reasoned. 'Would you prefer me to have told him outright that you're Paddy's daughter?'

Kelly hesitated, not really knowing what she preferred.

Ryan watched her biting her lip and he added quietly, 'Listen, if you want, I'll tell him.'

'No, don't bother.' She covered her uncertainty with a shrug. 'I might as well rattle around in the closet a while longer.'

'The closet?'

'You know—the family skeleton. That's me, isn't it?'

For once, he seemed amused by her flippancy. 'Well, one of them, maybe, but it's hardly a unique position. In fact, you're not even the only bastard in the family.'

Something in his manner had Kelly reaching the right conclusion before rejecting it. 'You don't mean *you*, do you?'

He inclined his head. 'I don't know why you're so surprised. From memory, you've called me that on at least one occasion,' he stated drily.

'I wouldn't have if I'd realised,' Kelly claimed quite seriously. 'I know how it feels—when you really are one, I mean.'

'Yes,' Ryan grimaced in reply, and for a moment they exchanged a look of understanding. Then he smiled with irony. 'Well, at least we've got *something* in common!'

'True,' Kelly agreed, smiling a little too, though it was scarcely the sort of thing on which friendships were based.

And yet, as they began walking towards the terminus exit, she wondered what *had* been his motive in admitting his illegitimacy. Surely not to make her feel better about her own?

Finding no answer, Kelly gave up on the problem as they emerged in bright sunlight to find Jeff already waiting with their transport. Not dressed for travelling in an open vehicle, she was relieved to discover the 'best jeep' was a Land Rover, recent in vintage, if coated in a film of dust. She climbed into the rear, leaving the men to sit together.

A sign indicated the actual town of Katherine was some ten miles from the airport, but they turned in the opposite direction, and within minutes it seemed they'd left civilisation behind.

Spirits sinking, Kelly stared out at the passing scenery: scrub grass and low trees, earth mounds and bare rock, wild country with a stark, desolate air. Though she had adapted to several different environments in her short lifetime, none had ever felt quite so alien and inhospitable at first sight. Compared to the soft, green shades of Ireland, it appeared an almost God-forsaken place, this Outback.

Of course, she wasn't going to express such an opinion, nor show any misgivings if the cattle station turned out to be as primitive. That would be just the reaction Ryan would anticipate from the 'spoilt film star's brat' he'd once accused her of being. And somehow she intended proving him wrong on that score, if none other.

To get an idea of where they were, she dug out a guidebook from her crammed flight bag. On the detailed map inside the cover, she eventually managed to find Katherine, one hundred and twenty miles inland from Darwin and the coast. Two main routes branched southwards from the town, but she assumed they had taken neither. She waited for a lull in the men's conversation and, leaning forward with the map, asked Ryan the general location of the cattle station. He pointed to an area directly south of Katherine.

And Jeff supplied, 'We're taking the Track.'

'The track?' Kelly echoed.

'He means the Stuart Highway.' Ryan traced the coast-to-coast road from Darwin to Adelaide, passing through the very centre of Alice Springs. 'Locals call it the Track.'

'And when do we join it?' Kelly asked in all seriousness.

Ryan frowned, then said drily, 'We're on it now.'

'*This* is the main highway?' She looked askance at the road.

'What did you expect—a three-lane motorway?' he laughed shortly.

The flush on Kelly's cheeks betrayed her even as she mumbled back, 'No, of course not. I just thought it would be busier.'

Unconvinced, he slanted her a mocking smile. All of a sudden, he seemed to find her a source of amusement, and Kelly wasn't sure if she liked it.

More kindly, Jeff put in, 'Well, it is at times,' and as if to support the claim they passed two vehicles in quick succession, a heavy supply truck and a busload of tourists.

But they saw few others in the next hundred miles and eventually, when Ryan took over the driving, they turned off the main highway on to a dirt road. Then it soon became evident why the Land Rover was dust-coated and had two spare wheels strapped to its roof-rack. Speeding over the rutted surface, Kelly learned to be more appreciative of the sealed highway they'd left behind.

The men seemed barely aware of the condition of the road as they discussed events during Ryan's absence. Kelly listened in, hoping to learn something of the homestead. But the conversation centred on mustering operations and cattle losses and problems with unreliable machinery. Almost as an afterthought, Jeff mentioned that two stockmen had rolled over a jeep, first assuring Ryan that the vehicle had survived the experience before giving an account of the men's injuries. From Ryan's equally casual reaction to the story, Kelly could only assume such accidents weren't rare.

They'd been on the dirt road some considerable time when they met a truck travelling in the opposite direction. The driver hooted his horn, and recognised Ryan with a broad grin as the two vehicles passed.

'Are we near the station?' Kelly asked afterwards.

Turning in his seat, Jeff confirmed, 'The homestead itself is just another five miles or so, but we've been on Kilconnell Downs for the last twenty.'

Kelly's eyes widened in surprise. 'How big *is* the station?'

Jeff paused, perhaps waiting for Ryan to volunteer the information. When he didn't, the head stockman went on, 'Well, this section's almost two thousand square miles. But we run a couple of smaller stations nearer Katherine, and they bring it up to about four.'

Kelly's eyes widened further. Four thousand square miles sounded an awfully large expanse of land.

'Is that big... by Australian standards, I mean?' she enquired of Jeff.

He grinned at the question, but didn't get a chance to reply before Ryan cut in, 'There's bigger. And without the cattle, the land itself isn't worth much.'

'Really?' Kelly hadn't supposed it was. In fact, she had difficulty believing the wiry-looking shrub even supported cattle.

'Beef prices are rock-bottom, too,' Ryan added, seemingly intent on presenting the worst of pictures.

And Kelly began thinking she was being informed, less than subtly, that, if she'd come looking for a prospective goldmine, she hadn't found it.

Inclined to tell him what he could do with his tinpot empire, she was beaten to a response by Jeff, who claimed, 'Kilconnell's still one of the most profitable stations in the Territory, though,' and thereby completely contradicted the impression Ryan was trying so hard to create.

Which, in turn, appealed to Kelly's wayward sense of humour, making her say, 'Well, that's a relief. Sure, I was beginning to think it all blarney I'd heard about these rich Australian relations of mine.'

Jeff saw it as a joke and laughed.

Ryan didn't. There was nothing amused about the look he threw her as their eyes clashed in the rear-view mirror.

Ignoring it, she returned Jeff's grin instead. At least *he* realised when a person was kidding.

It was also Jeff who provided a commentary when they eventually approached the homestead, and he observed her bemusement at finding, not a handful of farm buildings, but virtually a small town, built round a central piazza of bare ground.

The actual stockyards, an immense array of tubular steel, lay on the far side from the living quarters. Understandably, Kelly thought, for even from a distance she could hear the lowing of cattle and see the swirls of choking dust churned up by their hooves.

Skirting the near side, they first passed two parallel rows of bunkhouses for the stockmen, basic in structure, but stone-built and, according to Jeff, of a better standard than on many stations in the Territory. Along from these was an open-air recreational area, cement-based with a roof of wire mesh; here the men gathered to talk over a beer in the evening.

Next came a large corrugated shed for the station's variety of vehicles, followed by a communal dining-hall, meat store and cook house. Then there was a gap before the offices, used for the paperwork side of running a cattle station, and another, separating them from more living accommodation, this time individual apartments for the married and senior personnel like Jeff.

Till finally, at the top end of the square, perhaps a hundred yards from the rest of the homestead, stood a long brick bungalow in grounds surrounded by wrought-iron fencing. A sprawling rather than stylish house, it gained some charm from a wide sloping veranda and the stretch of lawn in front. As they drew up beside the fence gate, Jeff explained the garden only survived through frequent watering from an Artesian bore. Kelly wasn't quite sure what an Artesian bore was—presumably a well of sorts—but she didn't ask.

In fact, she was no longer really listening to the stockman's commentary. For, at their approach, a figure had appeared in the shadow of the bungalow doorway—the man she'd come to meet, this stranger who was suddenly her father. And she found that, despite days of thinking about it, she wasn't prepared for the moment. Not prepared at all.

She sat frozen in her seat while the luggage was unloaded and Jeff went ahead with a couple of suitcases. She still made no move to get down when Ryan came round to hold open her door.

He leaned inside the Land Rover, an impatient look on his face, but it faded when he saw the almost sickly pallor of Kelly's. She glanced very briefly at him, then away.

'Scared,' he said quietly, more statement than question.

It took time in coming, but eventually she gave a small, wordless nod.

'Of disappointing or being disappointed?' he went on to ask.

At this, Kelly turned to stare at him in surprise. She hadn't expected him to understand, but it seemed he did. 'Both, I suppose,' she admitted in a shy-sounding voice.

Her obvious uncertainty disarmed Ryan. Returning her stare, he saw what his father would see—a bright, beautiful girl with a look of innocence in her wide green eyes. And for a moment he wished the image were true, if only for Paddy's sake.

'Don't worry, it'll be all right—I promise,' he said, reaching inside to help her down.

For once, Kelly did not question his behaviour. Nor did she shrug away as he guided her through the gate and up the path towards the house. Perhaps it was just his familiarity in an otherwise unfamiliar world, but she accepted the reassurance offered by his arm, resting lightly on her waist. Without it, she might have turned and fled from that ominous figure, watching in the doorway.

Not until they neared the veranda did he step out of the shadows and make Kelly's imaginings appear, all at once, absurd.

For, silver-haired and still handsome, ominous was the last word anyone would apply to Paddy Devlin. If he hadn't rushed forward to greet them, it was due solely to a cumbersome plaster, encasing a broken ankle. That he welcomed her became evident from the very first look they exchanged, and the wealth of tenderness in his eyes.

Kelly stared back in wonder. The resemblance *was* striking—from cleft chin and wide, expressive mouth, to the head of thickly curling hair. Yet it made him no less of a stranger to her.

By the time Ryan led her up the porch steps, her nervousness had returned. For a moment she stood, stiff with embarrassment. Then she took refuge in politeness, extending a hand without realising that the sheer formality of the gesture might cause pain.

Paddy Devlin hid the fact well, and contented himself with gently squeezing the offered hand. A sensitive man, he understood her right to reserve.

To lessen the strain, he admitted humorously, 'Sure, I've been rehearsing a grand speech all afternoon. And now, would you believe, I can't remember a word of it?'

'I know the feeling,' Kelly found herself confiding, drawn by his surprisingly strong Irish accent.

And when he added, 'But you're a sight for sore eyes, Kelly girl, so you are,' in that soft brogue, the sentiment came over as wholly natural.

Touched, rather than embarrassed, Kelly answered with a small, shy smile.

When he turned to give Ryan a hard, affectionate shoulder-hug, he said more gruffly, 'Thank you, son. Thank you.'

It seemed unlikely Ryan would regard her presence as anything to be grateful for, but he responded to the rough male embrace with a spontaneity and warmth that surprised Kelly considerably.

Then her attention was drawn by Jeff's reappearance on the veranda. Alongside him stood a tall, blonde-haired woman of about thirty, beaming a welcome at Ryan. She was dressed in a plain summer frock that failed to hide a generously curved figure.

Before Kelly had time to wonder who the woman was, Paddy supplied the introductions, 'Kelly, I'd like you to meet Meg Donaldson, our housekeeper. And Meg,' he continued, smiling broadly, 'this beautiful girl here is my daughter, Kelly.'

CHAPTER SIX

No ONE smiled back.

Meg Donaldson stared at Kelly, an initial look of shock gradually turning into something that seemed oddly like satisfaction. Jeff stared too, obviously bewildered and trying to work out how she'd been promoted from second cousin to daughter in the space of a few hours. As for Ryan, he confined himself to an exasperated mutter at his father's frank, thoughtless honesty.

And Kelly's own reactions? Well, gossip apart, by claiming her outright, Paddy Devlin made her feel that at least *he* wasn't ashamed of her existence.

'What a surprise!' Meg Donaldson was the first to recover. 'Why, I never even knew you had a daughter.'

'Didn't you?' Paddy said, as if it was common knowledge, and offered no further explanation, despite the open curiosity in her gaze.

It was Ryan who supplied, 'Kelly was brought up in Ireland by her mother's people,' presumably to account for her absence from the scene.

After a moment's consideration, the woman nodded in reply, 'I see.'

But poor Jeff was still struggling to sort out fact from fiction. 'So she's really your sister?'

'No!' Ryan denied with resounding abruptness, an echo of Kelly's own feelings.

Jeff looked more confused than ever. 'But if Paddy's her dad——' he began to reason.

At this point, Meg Donaldson cut in, 'She's not his real sister, Ryan means,' and darted the stockman a silencing glare.

It had the desired effect, a slow flush creeping up Jeff's face as he finally remembered Ryan was adopted.

Though he'd been told the fact by one of the older men, he'd long since lost any consciousness of it.

Realising now that he was on awkward ground, he mumbled back, 'Yes, well...I'll go fetch the other cases,' and beat a hasty retreat.

'I hope I didn't speak out of turn,' Meg Donaldson added to Ryan.

He shook his head, then awarded her a late smile before suggesting, 'Perhaps you could show Kelly her room, Meg.'

'Yes, of course,' the Australian woman smiled back, and Kelly, sent an apologetic look by Paddy, reluctantly followed her inside.

The first thing she noticed was the bungalow's coolness. She thought it might be due to the stone-tiled flooring, until she caught the hum of air-conditioning. Evidently they enjoyed more home comforts than Ryan had implied.

They walked along a hallway to the back of the bungalow and the wide corridor which ran its length.

Meg nodded to the right. 'The general rooms are on that side, but I imagine you'll want to freshen up before you have the full tour.'

'Yes, thanks,' Kelly responded to the woman's first friendly overture.

'These are all bedrooms,' she relayed as they took the left fork in the corridor. 'Yours is at the far end.'

Trailing after her, Kelly caught a glimpse of a couple of other rooms in passing. They were austere in their plainness—bare stone flooring, walls plaster-white and the furniture of a heavy, old-fashioned kind. Thinking hers would be similar, she was almost astonished by the difference in it.

Instead of stone tiling, a soft powder-blue carpet covered the floor and complemented the light, modern cane furniture in the room. Draping the bed was a cotton quilt, patterned with blue wild flowers on a white background. It matched the blinds at two windows and the cushion on a large basket chair. And, if the walls were plaster, their bareness was relieved by a series of pretty prints.

'It's lovely,' Kelly said, genuinely charmed by the room.

'It should be,' Meg returned on a much drier note. 'The last month Paddy's been flying up and down to Darwin to arrange everything. Not that he let on why, but I assume he knew all the time you were coming?' she finished with a questioning lift.

'Yes, he did,' Kelly confirmed, feeling guilty as she weighed the attention that had gone into preparing for her arrival against the almost careless way she'd agreed to come.

'Just this morning he said Ryan might be bringing home a guest,' Meg Donaldson continued, eyes narrowed curiously.

'Really?' Kelly murmured, politely non-committal.

'I suppose that's why Ryan went to Europe—to accompany you on this trip,' she speculated.

This time, Kelly didn't comment at all. Instead she lifted one of her suitcases on to the bed and began to unpack, hoping to divert any direct questions.

An unsuccessful tactic, as Meg went on, 'You know, I can't get over Paddy having a daughter! How long has it been since your last visit, dear, if you don't mind me asking?'

Kelly did mind, for the 'dear' sounded condescending, and she'd already had enough of Ryan treating her like a child without this woman following suit.

'Actually, this is my first visit,' she stated coolly.

'Well, fancy that,' Meg Donaldson replied with what had to be the phoniest of surprised tones.

'Yes, fancy,' Kelly repeated somewhat archly before noticing Paddy Devlin by the door, arm crutches now taking the weight off his plastered foot.

Unaware of him, the other woman went on, 'No wonder old Paddy's been killing the fatted calf,' and directed a contemptuous glance round the newly decorated room. Contemptuous, at least, until she spotted 'old Paddy' in the doorway. Then her face went a deep, unbecoming red.

'Well, Meg,' he eventually spoke up, 'if it's the fatted calf I'm after killing, maybe you'd best be off and see how it's cooking.'

A wry dismissal, it had Meg Donaldson's mouth tightening in a thin, furious line. But, if aware of her anger, Paddy took little notice, stumping past her to manoeuvre himself down on the basket chair. And, when the housekeeper finally flounced out of the room, he said to Kelly, 'By God, I've done it now. We'll be lucky if we're not eating burnt offerings for a week.'

He pulled a face at the prospect, and for a moment they laughed together, conspirators.

Then the laughter died away, leaving them to stare at each other in silence, with nothing to say as strangers and, at the same time, so many things as father and daughter. Only, twenty years could scarcely be bridged in a single moment.

Feeling it safer to stick to the subject of Meg Donaldson, Paddy resumed, 'I take it she's been asking some awkward questions?'

'She was beginning to,' Kelly nodded.

'My fault, I'm afraid,' Paddy said with a sigh. 'Ryan's right—I shouldn't have been so blunt out on the porch. Either that, or I should have explained the situation before you arrived.'

Conceding that Ryan might, for once, have a point, Kelly asked, 'Why didn't you?'

'Well, to be honest,' Paddy admitted reluctantly, 'I didn't want to tell anyone in case you didn't come. Even when Ryan telegraphed your arrival time from London, I was still worried you might change your mind at the last moment. Sounds silly now, I suppose.'

'Not really.' Kelly felt she should be honest, too. 'I *was* having doubts and, as Ryan will probably tell you, I wasn't very eager to come in the first place.'

'That's natural enough.' Paddy smiled a little sadly. 'I imagine it was more upsetting than anything—finding out about me so suddenly. Perhaps the kinder thing would have been to leave you believing Armand your father.'

'It's OK. I already half suspected he wasn't, from something my granny said once.'

'But your mother never told you about me?'

Shaking her head, Kelly said almost as consolation, 'Jay believed she was going to, though.'

'Jay?' he quizzed.

'Jason Rutherford. He was an old friend of Mother's . . . I've been staying with him since her death,' she relayed, watching for his reaction.

He simply nodded, 'I believe Ryan mentioned him in one of his telegrams.'

'Yes, I know.' Kelly's mouth pulled downwards. 'I know what he implied, too. But that's because he jumped to all the wrong conclusions. I mean, when he thought that Jay and I . . . well, that we . . .'

'There's no need to explain,' Paddy put in gently. 'I felt he must have misunderstood.'

'He did—*totally*!' she confirmed with emphasis.

'Well, I'm sure you set him straight.' He smiled at her spirited retort. 'So, how have you been getting along since then?'

This time, Kelly showed some restraint in replying, 'Perhaps you'd better ask him that.'

'I did,' Paddy admitted, chuckling slightly. 'And do you know what he said?'

'What?' Kelly doubted it would be pleasant.

'Word for word, he said, "Perhaps you'd better ask her that,"' Paddy quoted, evidently amused by the coincidence.

Kelly laughed too, seeing the funny side. It must have been the first time she and Ryan had been of the same opinion!

'Now, would I be right in thinking the two of you aren't always in such perfect agreement?' Paddy added wryly.

'Not always, no.'

'Well, never mind. It'll be different when you get to know each other better,' Paddy declared with smiling optimism.

'Maybe.' Kelly was much more sceptical.

But Paddy continued to smile as he levered himself out of the basket chair and, joking that dinner, if served at all, would be shortly after sunset, he left her to unpack.

The task did not take Kelly long, as there was ample wardrobe and drawer space for her two suitcases of clothes. She did it automatically, then lay down on the bed to turn over in her mind her first conversation with her 'father'. But, still travel-weary, she soon fell fast asleep.

It was dark outside when she woke. She rose quickly, discarding her crumpled clothes before having a hurried wash in the handbasin that was another new addition to her room. Then she changed into a simply cut dress of white linen and, again feeling very much an outsider, nerved herself to go looking for the rest of the household.

She walked down the corridor to the far side of the bungalow, and tentatively pushed open the first door on the right. It led into a lounge, the furniture heavy and old-fashioned, as in the bedrooms, but given a comfortable air by the extensive collection of books lining the walls. Though the room was deserted, she allowed herself some curiosity, crossing to the piano on which a set of photographs were grouped.

Her eyes were drawn first to the picture of Ryan Devlin as a youth, slightly blonder in the hair, but already showing signs of the arrogantly handsome man he was to become. Next to it stood a wedding photograph, the groom dressed in an Australian army uniform, the bride in a forties costume suit. The seriousness of their pose only highlighted how young Paddy Devlin and his wife had been when they had married.

Kelly skirted over other family groupings until her eyes were caught by a small photograph at the far end. Again of Ryan, but this time as a very young child, with an unbelievably angelic face. She picked up the silver frame and was smiling down at it when Meg Donaldson suddenly appeared in the doorway.

'Oh, *there* you are,' the Australian woman said, in a tone that suggested Kelly should have been elsewhere.

At any rate, she found herself explaining the obvious, 'I was just looking at the photographs,' while hastily resetting the one she was holding.

Meg Donaldson did not reply, but joined her at the piano and, very deliberately, re-angled the frame to a different position.

Kelly wondered how to take this gesture. It seemed as if more than the photograph was being put in its place.

'The men are waiting dinner for you,' the housekeeper announced crisply, and left Kelly to follow her down the corridor.

Kelly did so with reluctance, but when she entered the dining-room, Paddy Devlin smiled broadly from the head of the table and waved her into the chair on his right.

'I'm sorry if I've delayed dinner,' she murmured as she sat down.

'Not at all,' he replied warmly. 'We'd have woken you earlier, only Ryan thought it might be better to leave you to sleep the clock around.'

Kelly just bet he had. Seated at the opposite side of the table, a grim-faced Ryan had yet to acknowledge her, and she imagined he would have been quite happy to have her absent from the meal.

'Anyway, Meg's used to juggling mealtimes. And when it comes to cooking, there's no one to beat her,' Paddy went on, his smile switching to the housekeeper.

But the Australian woman's face remained stony.

Paddy tried again. 'You've only set three plates, Meg. Aren't you going to sit down with us? You're very welcome, you know.'

'No, thank you,' was sniffed back. 'I have to keep an eye on the dinner.'

Paddy frowned over the rebuff and, when he looked at Kelly, she gave a sympathetic shrug. To her mind, he had more than made up for any offence caused earlier.

'What's wrong with Meg?' Ryan asked after the housekeeper had bustled from the room.

'Wrong?' Paddy echoed with an innocent air.

Ryan wasn't fooled. 'Something's obviously upset her.' His eyes switched to Kelly, almost accusing her of being responsible. 'Normally she eats with us as a matter of course.'

'Well, perhaps we had a little disagreement earlier,' Paddy admitted. 'I'm afraid Meg was harassing Kelly a little bit.'

'Harassing?' Ryan questioned. 'That doesn't sound like Meg.'

'Not to you, possibly,' Paddy said with a slight smile. 'But then, Meg's always especially pleasant where you're concerned.'

'Is she? I haven't noticed.'

'No, for all her pains, poor Meg.'

Ryan's brows drew together. 'What's that supposed to mean?'

Kelly smiled down at her plate. She thought it perfectly plain what Paddy meant, though his only answer was a wry shake of the head before he turned his attention to his meal.

Ryan, however, wasn't about to drop the subject so easily, and remarked directing the words at Kelly, 'Well, whoever's at fault, I hope you'll make an effort to get on with Meg. Because without her, you'd find things pretty damn uncomfortable around here.'

Kelly doubted that, but confined herself to shrugging, 'I've barely said a word to the woman.'

'Maybe that's the trouble. In Australia we treat our servants as human beings, not inferiors,' he returned in a lecturing tone that had Kelly gritting her teeth.

'Really?' She feigned amazement. 'Well, forgive my ignorance. You see, in Ireland we don't have servants to treat either way.'

As a smart answer, it was one of Kelly's best. While she smiled in impudent satisfaction, Ryan's face went into rigid lines of anger. Explosion seemed imminent.

That was before Paddy stepped in, quickly trying to move the conversation on to safer ground by asking Kelly how long she'd actually stayed in Ireland.

It was an obvious distraction, but Kelly played along, and soon they were talking easily again, sharing impressions of the 'old country'—of people and places and customs that had hardly changed in forty years. And, despite almost a lifetime spent in exile, Paddy Devlin's affection for his birthplace appeared to be as strong as his accent. Yet he recognised his sentimentality for what it was.

'Of course, you have to be careful not to lyricise too much in front of our native-born Australians,' he warned, a wry glance including Ryan in this category, 'or they'll turn round and ask you why you ever left the Emerald Isle, if it was such a grand place. Then you'll be forced to admit that, for all its beauty, you were eager enough to trade a legacy of poverty for the promise of a new land,' he ended on a more serious note.

Kelly nodded in understanding. She knew that, in the past, emigration had often been the only choice for Ireland's poor.

'Why did you choose Australia?' she asked of Paddy.

'It was more of a case of it choosing me,' he admitted drily. 'You see, my father had an uncle who'd come out before the Great War. The family hadn't heard from him in years when he finally wrote, telling us of the grand farm he had.

'Anyway, a couple of letters were exchanged, and the next thing I know, my father's packing me off to Australia. Later I realised he wanted to give me the chance of a better life, but at the time—well, I was fighting with me last breath to get off that ship.'

Kelly smiled at the image. Out of the corner of her eye, she could see Ryan was smiling too, though he must have heard the story many times.

'How old were you?' she pursued, genuinely interested.

'Sixteen, and never been further than twenty miles from Ennistimon in me life,' he confided with a gently self-mocking air. 'Between sea-sickness and bemoaning my fate, a sorry sight I was when we landed in Darwin Harbour. And sorrier still when the lush farmland of my imagining turned into the hard, bitter earth of the Outback. As for the homestead, it was nothing but a collection of tin shacks in those days.' He shook his head at the memory.

'And your uncle—what was he like?' asked Kelly.

'A man of few words and an even shorter temper,' Paddy laughed in reply. 'When I finally arrived with the year's supplies, he looked me up and down as if I was part of the consignment, searched without success for some muscle in my arm, then suggested the devil take my father for the liar he was. It seems my age and physical condition had been somewhat exaggerated in the exchange of letters... Never mind, we liked each other well enough in time, and he left me Kilconnell and his dream of cattle,' Paddy said with a reminiscent smile.

Then conversation was suspended, as Meg Donaldson reappeared with the main course on a trolley. Still playing the chilly housekeeper for all she was worth, she removed their dirty plates in tight-lipped silence.

But Kelly felt that perhaps she should make some overture, so she smiled, 'The soup was delicious, Meg.'

It drew a very stilted, 'Thank you,' and absolutely no smile at all, as the housekeeper began to serve the meat dish.

This was hardly encouraging, but Kelly tried again, offering pleasantly, 'Here, let me give you a hand.'

However, before she could rise to help, the other woman sniffed, 'There's no need. I can manage perfectly.'

After that, Kelly gave up. She felt it must now be quite clear which one of them was behaving unreasonably.

Yet, when the housekeeper finally bustled from the room, Ryan had the nerve to say, 'You don't have to overdo it, you know.'

'*You* told me to make an effort,' she reminded him indignantly. 'Maybe you should tell your ladyfriend the same.'

'My *what*?' Ryan demanded, his voice rising.

'You heard.' Kelly shrugged in the careless manner guaranteed to infuriate him further.

Again Paddy stepped in smartly. 'Now, let's not argue about Meg,' he appealed of both. 'It's just that her nose is slightly out of joint, having another woman round the place. I'm afraid she considers it as her domain.'

'As far as I'm concerned, it is,' Ryan stated shortly.

'Then, if that's the way you feel, why don't you do something about it?' Paddy countered, the hint of a smile in his voice.

'I was trying to,' Ryan claimed, only his thoughts were clearly on a different track as he directed at Kelly, 'OK, maybe you meant to be helpful. But it'd just be better if you left things to Meg. Good housekeepers are a rare breed in the Outback, and I wouldn't like her un-settled—imagining her position is under any threat. You understand?'

'Perfectly,' Kelly retorted, feeling she understood a sight more than he did.

Ryan still laboured the point. 'After all, if Meg quit, we might have to rely on you to do the cooking and cleaning for us,' he suggested with a dry laugh, ridiculing the idea.

Paddy laughed, too, before he noticed the flash of temper in Kelly's eyes. Then he put in kindly, 'Sure he's just teasing, Kelly love. We'd not have you wasting your time, slaving over a kitchen sink.'

But Kelly wasn't upset at the prospect of housework so much as at Ryan's obvious belief she was incapable of doing it. An entirely unfounded belief, for her Granny Cormack had taught her to cook, and in the last months, when the old lady had grown frailer, she'd virtually taken over the running of the house. She was quite certain she could rival Meg Donaldson's culinary efforts.

Only it seemed rather idiotic to say so. She wasn't in competition with the Australian woman. And what did it matter if Ryan considered her worse than useless?

'You'll be too busy enjoying yourself, I hope,' Paddy continued at her silence. 'The Outback is a fascinating place, not least in the character of its people.'

'How many actually live on Kilconnell Downs?' Kelly asked, anger curbed in the face of his pleasantness.

'Over sixty,' Paddy replied, and went on to give her little sketches of its inhabitants.

For a small community, it was very cosmopolitan, the station cook being, in Paddy's words, a mean, grizzly old Scotsman, the head bookkeeper a Vietnamese refugee, and the mechanic an American who had also drifted there after the war in south-east Asia.

Yet there was only half a dozen women and, apart from Meg Donaldson, they were all in their late forties or fifties. Apparently this was because the stockmen with young families were based on one of the Northern stations Jeff had mentioned, where the homestead had its own schoolhouse and teacher.

Encouraged by her interest, Paddy spent the rest of the meal explaining the general operation of Kilconnell Downs and the two subsidiary cattle stations they owned.

Afterwards, he took her out to sit on the veranda. The skies had turned dark but brilliantly clear, the night air mild. A string of street-lamps lit up the settlement, and stockmen could be seen in the distance, walking from the dining-hall down to the recreation area. From what Paddy had said, theirs seemed a very basic life—in the saddle from dawn to dusk driving cattle, the evening hours whiled away, playing cards or talking over a beer.

Kelly, however, knew better than to decry it. Through her mother she'd met rich, sophisticated people, able to do anything they wished—yet always bored, restless.

Possibly it was her years in Ireland that gave her a different outlook from Suzie who, while envying her Ryan's company, had declared a cattle station in the Outback as the 'living end'. Whatever the reason, Kelly could appreciate that, if lacking in luxuries, such an existence might offer a rare kind of contentment.

Of course, she didn't imagine there was a place for her here. In time, she might grow fond of Paddy Devlin; she suspected that wouldn't be difficult. In time, she might even come to love this wild, rugged country as he had. But, given all the time in the world, she knew she could never peacefully co-exist with Ryan Devlin.

Perhaps it was just as well she planned no more than a brief stay—a month or two, until her university entrance was decided. Then, assuming she'd passed, she would return to France and, with an advance on her mother's royalties for *Sunset Gold*, she could rent an apartment near the Sorbonne. If she'd failed, she still favoured the idea of returning to Paris, a city once home to her, where her language skills might help her find an interesting job. Either way, she regarded Kilconnell Downs as a purely temporary refuge.

Unfortunately, Paddy seemed to have a rather different view. As they sat chatting on the porch, he mentioned places they would visit together when his cast was removed, almost two months hence. He also talked of

REWARD! Free Books! Free Gifts!

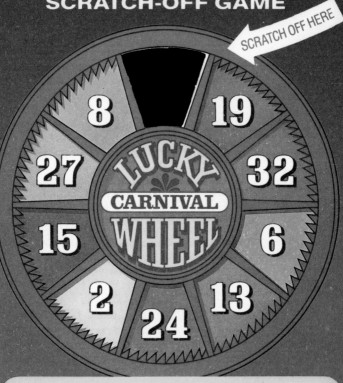

LUCKY PLAY HARLEQUIN'S

CARNIVAL WHEEL

SCRATCH-OFF GAME

SCRATCH OFF HERE

8   19

27   32

15   6

2   13

24

LUCKY
CARNIVAL
WHEEL

FIND OUT IF YOU CAN GET

FREE BOOKS AND A SURPRISE GIFT!

PLAY THE

LUCKY CARNIVAL WHEEL

scratch-off game
and get as many as
SIX FREE GIFTS...

HOW TO PLAY:

1. With a coin, carefully scratch off the silver area at right. Then check your number against the chart below it to find out which gifts you're eligible to receive.

2. You'll receive brand-new Harlequin Presents® novels and possibly other gifts—ABSOLUTELY FREE! Send back this card and we'll promptly send you the free books and gifts you qualify for!

3. We're betting you'll want more of these heartwarming romances, so unless you tell us otherwise, every month we'll send you 8 more wonderful novels to read and enjoy. Always delivered right to your home. And always at a discount off the cover price!

4. Your satisfaction is guaranteed! You may return any shipment of books and cancel at any time. The Free Books and Gifts remain yours to keep!

NO COST! NO RISK!
NO OBLIGATION TO BUY!

FREE! DIGITAL CLOCK/CALENDAR!

You'll love this lucite digital quartz clock! The changeable month-at-a-glance calendar pops out and can be replaced with your favorite photograph. This stylish clock/calendar can be yours FREE when you play the "LUCKY CARNIVAL WHEEL" scratch-off game!

CLAIM YOUR FREE GIFT. MAIL THIS CARD TODAY!

PRINTED IN U.S.A.

More Good News For Members Only!

When you join the Harlequin Reader Service, you'll receive 8 heartwarming romance novels each month delivered to your home at the members-only low discount price. You'll also get additional free gifts from time to time as well as our monthly newsletter. It's ''Heart to Heart''—our members' privileged look at upcoming books and profiles of our most popular authors!

If offer card is missing, write to: Harlequin Reader Service, 901 Fuhrmann Blvd., P.O. Box 1867, Buffalo, NY 14269-186 the Wet season, as if he expected her to be still there when it began in November.

Knowing she wouldn't be, Kelly felt she should tell him now. However, just as she was searching for the right words, Ryan came round the pathway from the back of the bungalow and she forgot entirely what she'd been about to say, instead staring, open-mouthed, at the woman glued to his side.

Pinched expression gone, her face lit up by a smile, the transformation in Meg Donaldson was little short of amazing. It could have been a different person.

'G'night, Paddy,' she called up as they passed by the foot of the veranda steps, then an even more amazing, if slightly stiffer, 'G'night, Kelly.'

'G'night, Meg,' Paddy smiled back.

''Night,' Kelly echoed the greeting too, rather late, for the couple were already half-way to the garden gate.

She turned her head, to find Paddy chuckling quietly to himself. 'Obviously it wasn't *our* efforts that were needed,' he observed in an undertone.

'Obviously,' Kelly agreed, wondering how Ryan had effected the change. She watched the couple walking towards the staff quarters and asked, 'Doesn't Meg stay in the bungalow?'

'Not yet, she doesn't.' Paddy slanted her a wry smile. 'But that's what she's been working on.'

This time, Kelly did not comment. It was fairly plain what Paddy was hinting at. What wasn't so plain was why she should dislike the idea of Meg Donaldson as mistress of Kilconnell Downs.

'The main problem is Ryan.' Paddy lowered his voice to confide, 'Between you, me and the gatepost, she's having a devil of a job getting him to the altar. Three years she's been at it, and personally I think if he's not in love with her by now, he never will be. What do you think?'

Kelly hesitated, reluctant to voice any opinion, and was almost relieved when the sound of approaching footsteps warned them of Ryan's return.

'You weren't long,' Paddy remarked as he joined them on the veranda.

'No,' Ryan agreed, typically unforthcoming.

Paddy, however, wasn't put off as he added with a speculative air, 'Still, Meg appeared to be in a better mood.'

'Once I explained things to her,' Ryan confirmed, his gaze switching briefly to Kelly.

Presumably she was the main 'thing' explained. She just wondered what he'd told his ladyfriend about her. Nothing good, that was for certain.

'I suppose people are bound to be curious,' Paddy sighed, glancing in apology at Kelly. 'I'm afraid you'll be getting some odd stares in the next few days. That can't be helped. But you must come and tell me if anyone deliberately upsets you.'

'Yes, all right,' Kelly agreed to please him, knowing full well she wouldn't do it.

'Well, I'll be off to bed,' he went on to announce and, before either could offer him a hand, rose to balance agilely on his crutches.

'I'll come with you,' Kelly volunteered, standing up to open the screen door.

'No, no, I'll manage. You stay and keep Ryan company.' He smiled at both of them, then, with a last goodnight, disappeared inside.

Kelly felt almost obliged to sit down again, though Ryan didn't look in the least need of company as he continued to lounge against the veranda. She checked her watch and decided to give it ten minutes before she followed Paddy inside.

Ryan saw the gesture, and realised she couldn't wait to get away from him. It was hardly surprising after their arguments over the dinner table. But he still felt angry, as he had for much of the evening.

It had started when he'd shared a beer with his father before the meal. Naturally, Paddy had been full of the girl—of how lovely she was, and how well mannered, and nicely spoken, and obviously bright. Ryan had listened to this catalogue of virtues with some forbearance. What had angered him was the gentle lecture that had followed, on looking for the best in people and not being too quick to judge a situation.

At first the point had escaped him, until his father had directly referred to the unfortunate *mistake* he'd made about Kelly and the old family friend who'd so kindly cared for her since her mother's death. Then he'd had to bite on his tongue to stop himself telling his father in precisely what manner this 'old family friend' had been 'caring for her'.

For Ryan was quite sure he'd made no mistake. He just had to remember her and Rutherford and the embraces they'd exchanged at Nice airport. It hadn't been so much a farewell scene as a three-act opera. Then there was the *little* parting present the man had given her—a platinum bracelet in a Cartier box, suggesting a price-tag Ryan couldn't have afforded even if he wanted to. And he definitely didn't, though it had annoyed the hell out of him.

It had annoyed him tonight, too, when he'd noticed it on her wrist. He'd wondered what she'd have said if he'd drawn Paddy's attention to the 'trinket'. No doubt she'd have convinced him it was a run-of-the-mill present among her circle of friends.

Watching her over dinner, Ryan suspected she'd be able to convince his father of just about anything. The rapport between them was already much stronger than he'd expected. And stronger, too, was the resentment he felt.

He couldn't decide exactly what he resented. After all, he'd come to terms with the girl's existence long ago.

He recalled how shocked he'd been initially. He'd looked up to his father so much, believing him infallible. And suddenly, there, in that hotel lobby, he'd been confronted by a different man, someone with weaknesses.

At first he'd refused to listen to any explanations, and had left his father to negotiate with Rhea Cormack while he flew home.

But when Paddy had returned, dispirited and depressed, Ryan's attitude had gradually changed to pity. If he'd felt offended at the existence of that pretty, dark-haired child, it seemed a small emotion compared to his father's devastation.

For months, Paddy had acted as if he'd forgotten his reason for living. He'd left the running of Kilconnell to Ryan or perhaps simply to chance. And he'd begun drinking.

It was then Ryan had really come of age, accepting the responsibility for both the station and his father. The station he'd just about managed. Paddy had been the hard part.

In the beginning, Ryan had been patient, pretending not to notice the drinking. Then he'd been protective, trying to ensure Paddy didn't do anything foolish in his drunken state, as he collected him from a variety of bars in Katherine. By that time, he'd no longer cared if his father had weaknesses like everyone else; he'd gone back to loving the gentle, amiable man who'd always treated him as a natural son.

But Ryan had recognised more drastic measures were called for, and one day he'd finally tried exploding—telling his father he couldn't manage the station, and wouldn't work his tail off any more so their profits might disappear down the throat of some drunk. He'd shouted and sworn and insulted Paddy into realising what was happening to him. And it had worked; Paddy had stopped drinking from that moment on.

But at times he'd relapse a little. Mostly that had been when the girl's photographs came. Sent on an erratic basis, they'd stopped when she was fourteen. After that there was the occasional letter, always with some excuse why a visit to Australia was impossible that year.

It was quite plain, to Ryan at least, that Rhea Cormack would never let the girl come to them and, bound by a promise given at that meeting in Dublin, Paddy had not attempted to seek her out. Then they'd heard of her mother's death, and Paddy decided the promise no longer stood. The child needed them and must be brought home to Kilconnell Downs.

What could Ryan say? *He* realised the 'child' was now nineteen and, with her mother's money, was as likely to need them as a welfare handout. And the kind of girl he visualised wasn't going to call a dusty cattle station home. But, when Paddy had broken his ankle, he'd offered to go looking for her.

It had proved the right decision. At least he'd spared him the lurid tale of hotel rooms and ski instructors. And the girl herself had done a whitewash job on her relationship with Jason Rutherford. So wasn't it best to let him keep imagining her a little princess?

Ryan supposed it was, but he still disliked the idea of his father being deceived. Perhaps that was what he'd resented at dinner—how effortlessly she charmed, with her pretty ways and that quick, engaging smile.

He studied her now, as she sat with her head bent, ignoring him. There was a sullen set to her mouth and a restlessness to be gone, betrayed by her twisting and turning the bracelet on her wrist. He resented that too and, when she finally made a move to rise, he forestalled her.

'Paddy already seems fond of you,' he said with a cynical edge to his voice.

Subsiding in her seat, she matched it as she retorted, 'Amazing, isn't it?'

'Not really—you can be charming enough when you choose.'

'Thank you.'

'That wasn't intended as a compliment,' he added, quite unnecessarily.

'*Wasn't it?*' She feigned surprise and received an impatient look in return.

'I don't happen to regard charm as a quality,' he stated, grim-faced.

'Evidently,' Kelly couldn't resist commenting.

'What's that supposed to mean?' he demanded irritably.

With a shrug, she responded, 'Well, charm's hardly your ladyfriend's strong suit.'

This time she was awarded a positive scowl. 'If that's a reference to Meg, at least *she's* honest.'

'Implying I'm not?'

'Let's just say you didn't waste any time this afternoon, convincing Paddy you were Little Miss Innocent.'

Kelly's lips tightened at the sneer. 'If that's a reference to my relationship with Jay, I simply told Paddy the truth and, unlike you, he listened.'

'I'm sure he did.' Ryan gave a short, humourless laugh. 'In fact, I'm sure he made it dead easy for you. After all, it was exactly what he wanted to believe.'

'Whereas you always want to believe the worst,' accused Kelly.

'In your case, it seems the wisest course,' Ryan countered. 'However, you don't have to worry—I didn't disillusion him. Nor, for the record, did I tell him about your little escapade with the ski instructor,' he added in a derisive tone.

'That's big of you,' Kelly retorted, wholly sarcastic. She didn't see any reason to thank him for *not* spreading lies about her. 'So why the silence?'

'I've decided there's no point in hurting Paddy unnecessarily. I'll keep quiet about your past, provided you don't give him any other wrong ideas.'

'Like what?'

'Like how long you're staying, for instance.'

'Oh?' Kelly arched a brow. 'And how long *am* I staying? Perhaps you'd better enlighten me.'

'That's up to you,' he shrugged indifferently. 'Just don't go raising his hopes that you intend making this your home.'

'For all you know, I might,' she said out of sheer devilment.

It drew another humourless laugh. 'No way! You'll be off as soon as you've got what you came for.'

Kelly frowned, slow to catch on to his meaning. She'd forgotten the economics lecture he'd given her earlier.

'And I doubt it's going to be long before you worm your way round Paddy,' he went on, his mouth curving in distaste. 'But I might as well warn you now. Most of his capital is sunk into the station, so I wouldn't be too greedy.'

Angry colour flooded Kelly's cheeks. 'You really think I'm after money?' she demanded, her indignant tone a denial in itself.

'Yes,' he answered flatly. 'Either that or a share in this place.'

'This God-forsaken hole—you must be joking!' Kelly said with all the scorn she could muster. 'I wouldn't have it as a gift. And with regards to money, anything I wanted, I could get from Jay. In a year he probably earns more than your tinpot empire could in five.'

Ryan's eyes hardened at the insult. If he loved anything, it was Kilconnell Downs.

'Then maybe you should have stuck with him if he was so generous,' he grated back. 'Tell me—how did he pay for your services? By the hour or the minute?'

The crudity of the question shocked Kelly. 'Don't be disgusting!' she threw at him and rose to her feet.

But Ryan also moved, crossing from the veranda railing to block her path to the door. 'By the minute, I expect—at his age,' he added brutally.

'Just shut up!' Kelly hissed in reply.

'No, I want to know.' He grabbed her arm when she would have passed him. 'What was it like, going to bed with that old man? Letting him paw at you, letting him make love to you...if you can call it that.'

But instead of having a withering effect, his contempt fuelled Kelly's temper. Instinct told her how to hurt back as she retorted, 'A damn sight better than being pawed by you, that's for sure. At least Jay doesn't go around forcing his attentions on women. *He* doesn't have to,' she finished pointedly, and the words seemed to echo in the long moment's silence that followed.

Then Ryan demanded, 'Meaning I do?' in a dangerously low voice.

Kelly failed to heed any warning, continuing rashly, 'Well, you hardly imagine I was willing that day at the pool.'

'Like hell you weren't!' he growled in response. 'Maybe you put up a token struggle in the beginning, but that's all it was. I could have had you right there, if I'd wanted.'

'That's a dirty lie!' Kelly flared, at the same time trying to jerk free from his hold.

But he caught her other arm and pulled her body to his. 'Is it? Let's see, shall we?'

For a second Kelly didn't understand the threat, not until his head started descending. Then it was too late to turn away.

It was a brutal kiss, a clash of teeth and lips and wills, without the remotest connection to love or affection. If he'd struck her, it would not have better conveyed the desire to hurt that drove him.

Nor was there anything token about Kelly's resistance. First she tried to twist her mouth from his, but a hand was thrust in her hair, forcing her head back and making it impossible to move. Then she tried straining away from him, her hands pushing furiously at his chest, but that, too, proved a useless struggle, for she was small and slight and had little strength against his powerful build. So finally, in sheer temper, she drew a leg back to give a vicious kick to his shins.

From his grunt of pain it was on target.

'You little bitch!' he swore as he pushed her almost violently away.

'Y-you promised,' she stammered, a little frightened by his reaction. 'You s-said you wouldn't touch me again.'

'You asked for it!' he accused in a low, harsh rasp, and, without giving her a chance to reply, turned on his heel.

Kelly watched as he took the veranda steps in a couple of strides, before heading towards the homestead buildings. She watched until he disappeared round the side of the living quarters. After that, her imagination took over.

She saw him knocking on Meg Donaldson's back door. Being welcomed with open arms. Kissing the older woman as he had never kissed *her*.

She shut her eyes before the images could become more intimate. She didn't care what he did with the Australian woman. It was nothing to her. Absolutely nothing.

She held on to that thought, repeating it to herself as she went inside, and undressed for bed and lay down in the dark to sleep.

But it made no difference. The tears still came.

CHAPTER SEVEN

THE next day, Paddy took her on a guided tour of the homestead, propelling himself agilely round on crutches.

Their first stop was the huge steel labyrinth of stock-yards, where cattle were being mustered. Compared to the placid cows Kelly was used to seeing in Ireland, they were fierce-looking specimens, and the skill of the stockmen was impressive as they wheeled their horses amid stamping, protesting steers and towers of choking dust. A hard, dirty task, they tackled it with grim-faced satisfaction.

When they'd finished, Paddy introduced her, again quite openly claiming her as his daughter. This time there were no shocked stares, suggesting news of her arrival had already been broadcast by Jeff or Meg Donaldson. Instead, the younger stockmen acknowledged her with diffident smiles, while the older, more confident ones complimented Paddy on her looks.

It was the same story when they crossed to the far side of the homestead to call in at the offices and married quarters. The men were unfailingly pleasant. The women, if curious, hid it well and, unlike Meg Donaldson, made her feel welcome.

Kelly realised that the warmth of their greeting was a measure of their liking for Paddy. Naturally they must have wondered how he had suddenly produced a grown-up daughter. But no one asked for explanations, and Paddy apparently didn't see any need to give them.

Kelly followed his lead, not anxious to advertise her background, either. It wasn't that she was ashamed of it. She just wanted to be taken at face value, to be liked or disliked for herself, not as Rhea Cormack's daughter, with all the prejudices that entailed.

At any rate, that first day set the pattern for the next week. In the mornings she would accompany Paddy on his rounds of the yards and offices. In the afternoons they'd sit on the veranda, watching the world go by. They talked of many things as they got to know each other, but, if daily Kelly meant to admit she wasn't staying long, the moment never seemed quite right.

During that period she saw little of Ryan. Intent on making up for his absence, he worked from dawn to dusk, and the only time they met was over the dinner table. There they exchanged bare civilities to hide the enmity created by their last bitter quarrel.

But whoever they imagined they were kidding, it wasn't Paddy. At first he sat on the sidelines, hoping the situation might improve. After a week, however, he realised he was being optimistic and decided to tackle Kelly.

'What happened between you and Ryan in France?' he asked her point-blank one afternoon when they were seated on the porch.

'Happened?' She gave him a blank, evasive look.

But Paddy wasn't to be put off so easily. 'Sure, something must have,' he insisted, 'the way you two treat each other.'

'I wasn't aware we treated each other in any particular way,' Kelly responded tonelessly, reluctant to confide her feelings for Ryan. Not when she didn't understand them herself.

'Perhaps that's my point,' Paddy pursued. 'I mean, at dinner you virtually ignore each other, and whenever I suggest he gives you a tour of the station, it's a race to see who comes up with an excuse first,' he added, a wry but accurate observation.

'All right, I suppose it's pretty plain we don't like each other,' Kelly finally admitted.

'Yes, but why?' Paddy frowned.

Kelly shrugged in return, 'Well, he's bound to resent me because of your relationship with Mum.'

For a moment Paddy looked bewildered, as if he hadn't considered such a possibility. 'Ryan's said that?'

'Not in so many words,' Kelly replied, 'but he's made some nasty comments about her. I suppose he blames her for trying to break up your marriage.'

'Oh, that can't be,' Paddy denied, still with an air of puzzlement. 'Marie and I were separated years before I met your mother.'

It was Kelly's turn to look somewhat bewildered.

'Ryan didn't tell you,' Paddy concluded from her expression, and went on to quietly explain, 'My wife never really liked Outback life, and in the end moved back to Sydney when Ryan went there for secondary school. The arrangement was that he live with her during term and return to Kilconnell for holidays.'

'But if you were separated——' Kelly broke off, the accusation in her eyes plain enough.

'Why didn't I marry your mother?' Paddy said for her. 'I wanted to, Kelly. Believe me, I wanted nothing more. Only when I returned from Europe, Marie refused to even consider a divorce.'

'You could still have gone back for Mum,' Kelly pointed out, not so ready to forgive his desertion now.

'I meant to,' Paddy sighed, 'and over the years, how I wished I had! Because I never forgot—never really stopped loving her. I know it doesn't make up for what I did. Nothing can ... But don't think I didn't love her,' he appealed in deep, moving tones.

And Kelly's anger faded as she began to see things in a different perspective. The fact he hadn't returned had probably caused Paddy Devlin more pain and regret than it ever had her mother. She had gone on to another life, to the glamour and excitement of the film world. Would she really have swopped that for a cattle station in the middle of nowhere? Kelly doubted it very much.

'You must have had a good reason for not going back,' she said quietly.

'At the time it seemed so,' Paddy confirmed. 'I'm afraid Ryan overheard us discussing the divorce and it led to problems.'

Kelly's curiosity was roused. 'What sort of problems?'

'You do know he was adopted?' Paddy asked and, at her nod, continued, 'Well, Ryan himself didn't—not until then. I remember we'd ended up arguing over the failure of our marriage. Marie always blamed it on us not having any children of our own, and we were too busy re-opening old wounds to notice Ryan, listening in the doorway,' he admitted with a touch of shame.

Kelly remained silent, but she could picture the situation, and her heart went out to the fourteen-year-old boy, regardless of the man he'd become.

Paddy went on quietly, 'At first he just stood there, staring at us with a blank look on his face, as if we'd suddenly become strangers to him. Then he turned away, went to his room and locked the door.'

'Without saying anything?' Kelly put in.

'Not a word. Though that was always Ryan's way, even as a youngster. If something hurts, he bottles it up inside,' Paddy confided, before adding with a sigh, 'Of course, later he wanted to know who his real parents were.'

Kelly saw that, if he'd understood the fact, it had still hurt. 'Did you tell him?'

'Not immediately. You see his mother was actually Marie's younger sister,' he revealed. 'She'd come to live with us for a while and ended up pregnant by one of the stockmen. Not a bad chap—ready to marry her, at least. But Frances didn't want the life of the Outback or the responsibility of a child.

'So Marie went down with her to Sydney until Ryan was born, then brought him back to Kilconnell. The way it worked out, most people assumed he was ours, and though we planned on explaining the truth to him some time, there never seemed any urgency. Perhaps if Frances had kept in touch, we would have early on, but she dropped out of our lives from the moment she handed him over.'

'So Ryan didn't know her,' Kelly concluded.

Paddy nodded. 'And Marie was dead set on leaving things like that. For good reasons, too. However, Ryan kept badgering her until she lost her temper and told him where to find Frances.'

'What happened?' Kelly sensed it hadn't been pleasant.

'Well, he went off, then and there, to visit her,' Paddy sighed. 'She'd married some business tycoon and was living in a big house in the suburbs of Sydney. Ryan gave his name at the door, only to be told after some delay that she wasn't in. I suppose he knew it was a lie, because he waited at the gates until she came out in her car.

'The really bad thing was that, though she was on her own, she still didn't stop to talk to him. Instead, she phoned Marie, demanding he stay away from her. She didn't need to, however, because Ryan himself disappeared. Three months he was missing, hired on as an apprentice with some shearing crew, and though he eventually returned of his own accord, from that day, he's never mentioned her name,' Paddy relayed in grave tones.

And Kelly was left feeling bitterly hurt for Ryan. It seemed obvious how the reunion scene had gone—a now rich and respectable Frances regarding an illegitimate son as merely an embarrassment. It was also in sharp contrast to the way she had been welcomed in similar circumstances.

'Sometimes I feel the whole business made him lose trust in people,' Paddy confided sadly. 'Perhaps it's why he's never come close to marriage. That and myself, of course. I know I haven't set either of you the best of examples,' he admitted, his eyes holding a lifetime's regrets.

'Maybe you couldn't help it,' Kelly suggested, doubting he had ever acted maliciously. 'I can see now

why you didn't go back for Mum. I mean, you didn't
know about me, did you? And Ryan obviously needed
you more.'

'You're a good girl for understanding, Kelly, so you
are,' Paddy replied with a slight catch in his voice as he
reached over to give her hand a gentle squeeze. 'Sure,
with the mess I've made of my life, I ask myself what
I did to deserve such a grand pair of children. My only
wish is that the two of you will be friends.'

An impossible wish, Kelly still felt, as she said, 'I don't
think that's very likely.'

'But you're willing to try?' Paddy appealed.

Weakening a little, Kelly replied, 'Yes, all right,'
though she wasn't too sure what he expected. She was
almost certain Ryan would reject any friendly overtures
from her.

Yet later that day, when they all sat down to dinner,
Kelly put it to the test and, while Paddy sustained most
of the conversation, she volunteered the occasional
remark in Ryan's direction. The first time she did so,
she drew a surprised stare; the second, a suspicious
frown; and on the third, an unintelligible grunt in reply.
After that she gave up, deciding Ryan Devlin had about
as much social grace as the cattle with which he seemed
so fond of spending his time.

It was Paddy who persevered, saying, 'I hear you're
flying the Cessna up to the mustering at Simpson's
Creek.'

'Tomorrow, yes,' he briefly confirmed.

'In that case,' Paddy went on, 'I was thinking you
could take Kelly with you. Show her a bit of the station,
perhaps?'

Kelly's face fell at the suggestion.

So did Ryan's but, noticing her reaction, he must have
felt safe in shrugging, 'If she wants.'

'Kelly?' Paddy sent her an appealing glance.

She was caught two ways. She certainly didn't fancy a day of Ryan's company, and plainly the feeling was mutual. Yet she'd promised Paddy to make an effort.

So she murmured, 'Well, if there's room for me,' and left it to Ryan to invent some excuse.

Instead he just stared at her again, and Paddy put in quickly, 'Of course there is. So that's settled. When will you be leaving?'

'About seven,' Ryan answered, eyes still trained on Kelly.

Realising he was waiting for her to object to the early hour, she remained stubbornly silent. If he thought her incapable of getting up in time, she was going to show him.

And that she did, rising the next morning at six forty-five to appear, sleepy-eyed, at the kitchen table. Already there, Ryan looked up from his plate in surprise, while Meg Donaldson, seated at his side, shot her a resentful glance.

'I suppose you want breakfast,' the Australian woman muttered, barely polite as usual.

'Just coffee, but don't let me disturb you,' Kelly replied as she crossed to the coffee-pot warming on the stove. She helped herself, then sat at the far end of table.

'You should eat something,' Ryan told her. 'We have a long day in front of us.'

'I'd prefer not to.' Her stomach felt queasy enough at the sight of him breakfasting on rare steak.

'Suit yourself,' he said shortly. 'Just don't complain if you're hungry later.'

'I won't!' she snapped back, wishing he wouldn't talk to her as if she was five years old. Especially not in front of Meg Donaldson.

'Will you be home for dinner?' the older woman asked.

'I should think so. We'll be leaving the Cessna at the mustering camp and coming back in one of the trucks,' he replied, then, finishing off his meal, directed at Kelly in a much brusquer tone, 'Are you ready?'

'Would it matter?' she said under her breath as, not waiting for an answer, he stood up to put on his jacket and hat.

She trailed after him, slipping into her own denim jacket, for the early morning air was a little cool as they walked to the vehicle shed. The head mechanic drove them out to the runway, situated about a mile from the homestead. She sat in the back of the jeep, listening to the men's conversation.

The mechanic seemed to be warning Ryan of some new foibles the plane had developed in his absence. It was not exactly reassuring.

Her first sight of the plane, pitted with rust and dented in places, was even less so.

'What's wrong?' Ryan asked when he caught her expression.

'Nothing. Just that I can see why you're considering scrapping it,' she said drily.

'Scrapping it?' He frowned for a moment, then went on to explain, 'It's our *other* plane we're going to scrap. This one's perfectly sound.'

'Oh.' Kelly looked unconvinced.

And Ryan couldn't resist adding, 'Well, provided the wind's in the right direction and the fuel tank doesn't start leaking again.'

'What?' Kelly switched her horrified gaze from the plane to meet a pair of decidedly amused grey eyes. 'I suppose that's your idea of a joke,' she added crossly.

'You'd better hope so,' Ryan drawled as he went round to climb into the pilot's seat.

Pulling a face, Kelly made no move to follow until he leaned out of the passenger side to offer a helping hand. Then she deliberately ignored it and, gripping the edges of the doorway, hoisted herself into the plane.

The slight was noted with a tight-lipped glance, before he instructed curtly, 'Here. You'd better put this on.'

A fur-lined flying jacket was dumped in her lap. Eyeing it suspiciously, Kelly asked, 'Why?'

This time Ryan's look was exasperated. 'Why do you think?' he said and, before she could come up with some crazy answer, told her, 'So you won't be cold.'

'Oh!' Kelly registered this information with some surprise. She wouldn't have thought he'd care if she froze to death. 'Thanks,' she mumbled rather belatedly as she pulled on the leather jacket over her own.

Then, looking round her, she asked, 'How do I shut the door?'

'There isn't one. That's why you'll need the jacket.'

'I see,' Kelly said, though she didn't.

She assumed there must be a perfectly logical reason there was no door. She just hoped it wasn't to enable them to bail out more quickly in the event of problems.

Deciding it better not to enquire, she fell silent and watched while Ryan flicked down various switches to turn on the engine. Then she nervously gripped her seat as he began taxiing the plane down the rudimentary runway. She felt almost a sense of anticlimax when they finally took off, as smoothly as a bird.

It was Kelly's first flight in a light aircraft, and fear soon changed to exhilaration. They climbed to about four hundred feet and, with the doors off, she had a clear view of the land below. It still looked wild country to her, stark in its desolation. Though man had introduced cattle and shrub grass, he seemed to have barely left his mark. Yet there was something grand in its very loneliness, a sense of space and freedom not to be found in more civilised worlds.

Noticing her interest, Ryan remarked, 'You probably find the Outback even more inhospitable from the air.'

'I don't know. It does have a wild kind of beauty,' Kelly said, speaking her thoughts aloud.

Not expecting such an answer, Ryan glanced at her in some surprise. 'It isn't totally God-forsaken, then?'

'Sorry?' The allusion escaped Kelly.

'It's what you said the first night. That you had no interest in Kilconnell because you considered it a "God-forsaken hole,"' he recounted, and this time the words did have a familiar ring to Kelly.

'Yes, well...I was a little mad at the time,' she excused with a shrug.

It was such an understatement that Ryan almost laughed aloud. He could only wonder what qualified as a *lot* mad. Their last quarrel—the one she now dismissed so easily—had left him feeling raw and angry for days.

Yet he chose to follow her lead, saying, 'We both were. Let's forget it.'

'All right,' Kelly agreed, quite happy to drop the matter. After all, *she* hadn't raised it.

'Good.' He smiled briefly, then switched back to the relatively safe topic of scenery.

Handling the plane with ease, he pointed out various landmarks below—the contours of a dry riverbed, the occasional broken-down dwelling of an earlier settler, and everywhere, the tall pinnacle structures of earth formed by the Outback's large population of termite insects.

For once he appeared relaxed in her company, but Kelly suspected that was due to the subject, his comments revealing a total absorption in the land. He talked as if it was a living thing, and left her with the impression that he felt more for Kilconnell Downs than he ever would for any person.

An oddly disturbing idea, Kelly pushed it from her mind as she switched her eyes back to the scenery and exclaimed on the sudden view ahead, 'That isn't a *river*!'

'Well, it's not the Mississippi or anything, but we like to think so,' he answered drily.

'I wasn't criticising its size. I was just surprised. I thought any rivers dried up in your winter months,' Kelly explained, trying to prove she wasn't altogether ignorant.

'A lot do, yes. Fortunately the Simpson has a deep bed, though the water level can fall pretty low by the end of the Dry.'

'I suppose it gets topped up during the Wet.'

'And then some,' Ryan confirmed as they began to follow its course downstream. 'Looks a pretty sleepy affair now, but wait till you see it in full flood, when the rains come. It flows in a torrent then.'

Kelly peered down at the river again, trying to picture it in flood. She knew she'd be long gone before the rains came in November. And Ryan knew it too, his 'wait and see' merely a slip of the tongue.

Yet he continued to talk about the changes the Wet season brought to the landscape until Kelly began to wonder if she wasn't the only one Paddy had persuaded into making some effort towards more friendly relations.

'How far is it to the mustering camp?' she asked after they'd been flying for an hour.

'We're almost there,' he told her and began to drop the plane's altitude. 'In fact, that's it. Dead ahead.'

Kelly's eyes widened in surprise as the camp came into view. Conditioned by cowboy movies, she'd been expecting to see nothing more than a wagon and a campfire. Instead there was a conglomeration of trucks and jeeps and trailer vans, grouped near the river, and an expanse of steel stockyards, as yet empty of cattle, but as large as the complex on the station itself.

Ryan made a couple of passes over the yards, viewing their layout from the air. Then he landed in a clearing some distance away, and they waited for the jeep, approaching from the camp to collect them.

When the driver pulled up, he grinned widely at Kelly. It took her a second or two to recognise Jeff, the head stockman who'd met them at Katherine airport. Having not seen him round the station in the last week, she'd almost forgotten him.

Jeff, however, hadn't forgotten her, and was still grinning as he said, 'I didn't realise Ryan was bringing you out here.'

'He didn't realise himself until last night,' Kelly admitted with a touch of wryness.

'Well, I'm glad you came,' he replied warmly, then more diffidently, 'I mean, I'm sure you'll find it interesting.'

'I hope so,' she smiled back, barely conscious of the effect she was having on the young stockman.

But Ryan noticed as he cut into the conversation with a brusque, 'Let's go, Jeff, I want to get started.'

Jeff frowned, slightly taken aback by his friend's abruptness.

Kelly was less surprised. She had doubted Ryan's 'pleasant phase' would last long. And it was clearly over as he held open the jeep's passenger door for her, impatience in every rigid line of his face. She climbed into the rear, leaving the men to sit together.

'Any problems in setting things up?' he enquired as they drove towards the camp.

'Not as far as the yards are concerned. They're all ready. But I'm afraid we're minus a cook again.'

'Since when?'

'Since last night when Christy decided to go walkabout,' Jeff relayed with a grimace.

'To the nearest pub, I assume,' Ryan muttered back.

'Probably,' Jeff nodded, 'though he's been dry for almost a month now.'

'That must be a record for Christy. Well, when he comes back, give him his cards,' Ryan instructed without hesitation.

Listening to the exchange, Kelly was immediately in sympathy with the absent Christy.

Yet it seemed Jeff supported the decision as he replied, 'That's what I thought you'd say, so I sent Davidson up to Katherine to hire another cook.'

Ryan gave an approving nod before asking, 'What are you doing in the meantime?'

'Well, for breakfast we had leftovers from supper, which didn't taste all that good first time around. For lunch, it'll have to be the salted beef,' Jeff said with a distinct lack of enthusiasm.

'I suppose,' Ryan agreed, 'though the men aren't going to be too happy.'

'No, and I don't blame them. But what else can we do?' Jeff appealed as they drew up at the camp.

From Ryan's grunt, he had no solution to offer.

But Kelly had. After all, she could cook well enough, and it seemed selfish not to help out.

'I could make something if you like,' she leaned forward to offer.

It brought Ryan swivelling round in his seat. He looked at her in frank amazement for a moment, then he laughed, *'You?'*

'Yes, me,' she returned crossly.

'You can cook?' His tone remained incredulous.

'Well, I'd hardly offer if I couldn't,' she pointed out.

'That's true,' Jeff put in, slanting her a grin.

But Ryan went on suspiciously, 'Where did you learn—finishing school?'

'Partly—why?'

'It's just that cooking for some fancy dinner party is one thing, and cooking for twenty hungry stockmen is quite another.'

Kelly began to wonder why she'd bothered offering to help out. 'I imagine twenty hungry stockmen are a sight less picky about what they eat,' she responded. 'However, if you have no faith in me...'

'I do,' came from Jeff, as he saw the prospect of a decent meal slipping away. 'And Ryan's probably just worried about you mixing with the men. They can be a rough bunch at times.'

'I wouldn't mind,' she returned, doubting Ryan had considered her feelings at all.

'Ryan?' Jeff appealed to him for a final decision.

'Your choice,' he shrugged at Kelly, and waited until they'd stepped out of the jeep, to add in warning, 'Only don't expect them to be too polite if they don't like what you cook.'

'Not as polite as you, you mean?' she said with a guileless look.

It took Ryan a couple of seconds to recognise the sarcasm behind it, then his eyes narrowed angrily. But he did not retaliate. Instead he muttered to Jeff, 'You'd better show her where to find things,' and with that, stalked off in the direction of the stockyards.

The other Australian stared after him. 'He's not too keen on the idea. Perhaps we should forget it.'

'Not on your life!' Kelly retorted, her face a picture of stubbornness. 'I'm going to cook the best damn meal he's ever had, then hope he chokes on it.'

Unsure whether he should, Jeff couldn't help laughing. 'If I didn't know better, I'd say you meant that. Remind me never to get on your wrong side.'

'I will.' Kelly's quick smile showed she also had a right side, full of humour and charm.

It was the side that drew most people to her, and the head stockman was no exception. He took her to the mobile cookhouse containing a bottled gas stove, refrigerator and stores. Then he spent an inordinate amount of time explaining everything.

Not realising she was the attraction, Kelly began to feel that the stockman had been influenced by Ryan into thinking her stupid. When he threatened to give her yet another step-by-step guide on how to use the cooking stove, she said, 'It's all right. I think I've got it.'

'Well, if you're sure...' Jeff was still reluctant to depart. 'Now, you'll find the fresh meat——'

'In the fridge?' Kelly suggested, a smile softening the irony in her voice.

'Pretty obvious, I guess.' The stockman gave her an apologetic look.

'Sort of,' she agreed, still smiling. 'The only thing you haven't told me is *what* to cook.'

'Oh, anything—whatever's easiest.'

'Stew?'

'That would be great,' Jeff nodded, and with a last grin backed out of the trailer.

He was soon forgotten by Kelly as she rolled up her sleeves and got stuck in to preparing the meal. Catering for twenty, it took her ages just to slice and brown sufficient meat for the base of the stew. There were no fresh vegetables, either, but after digging around in a highly disorganised store cupboard she found a large tin of carrots and some dried onions. She mixed them generously with the meat, seasoned lightly, and left the stew simmering on the stove.

Then, with no time to bake proper bread, she made doughy biscuits in batches, preparing one lot while another was baking in the oven. She was just finishing the last batch when she heard voices outside the trailer.

'Bloody salt beef, I bet!' one stated in loud disgust.

'It's not,' another contradicted. 'Jeff said we were having a proper meal.'

'Stone me, Christy's not back, is he?'

'Not him. He'll still be in Katherine, nursing a hangover.'

'Then who's doing the cooking?'

'It'll be that woman,' put in a new voice, quieter than the rest.

'Woman? What woman?' was demanded by the first speaker.

'The one Ryan brought in the Cessna,' the quiet voice told him. 'And I'd stop bellowing, MacIver, or she'll probably take flight right out again.'

'I wasn't bellowing,' MacIver bellowed back. 'Just surprised, that's all. Never known Ryan to hire a female cook for camp before.'

'What's she like, Danny?' someone asked the quietly spoken stockman.

'Couldn't tell,' he replied. 'Only saw her from the back.'

'Well, one thing's certain, Ryan won't have hired her for her looks,' MacIver stated disparagingly. 'My bet is she'll be long in the tooth.'

'Suit you then, Mac,' was suggested, drawing a round of laughter from the rest.

MacIver took the ribbing in good humour, his laugh the loudest. 'She'll suit me as long as she can cook. So let's find out.' He walked up the steps of the trailer and, knocking on the door, called out, 'Cooee, missus. Grub ready?'

Till then Kelly had been waiting for the right moment to announce herself, and growing progressively more nervous about their reception to her cooking. The shout from the stockman did little for her confidence, but she could hardly ignore it.

Five mouths dropped open as she appeared in the doorway. And, for almost a full minute, five pairs of eyes stared at her in absolute silence.

The spell was finally broken by MacIver, a mountain of a man, with a complexion like leather. In what was, for him, a mumble, he said, 'Sorry, miss, didn't realise,' and at the same time he pulled off his slouch hat.

Kelly wasn't sure what it was he 'didn't realise', but she smiled at the sudden show of politeness.

'That's all right. And...um...grub is ready,' she confirmed, echoing his phrase and drawing an abashed grin from the Australian as he ducked inside the trailer.

Kelly ladled out a huge plate of stew for him and put three biscuits on the side. 'Is that enough?'

He nodded, 'Should be. Don't have much of an appetite till we start mustering.'

Kelly, thinking she'd been generous, wondered how much he could eat when he did have an appetite.

'Smells blood—blooming good,' he said, as if to make up for his earlier comments.

'I'd suspend judgement until you taste it,' Kelly suggested on a wry note.

'"Suspend judgement"...rightio.' He repeated her words with a quizzical look, then retreated down the steps to confide to the rest, 'Talks bloody fancy for a cook, but I reckon she's a goer.'

Overhearing the comment, Kelly didn't know if a 'goer' was complimentary or insulting, but she didn't have time to worry about it as the men began filing in for their meal. Like MacIver, most were stricken with shyness in her presence, mumbling their thanks. She'd just served the last when Jeff reappeared, all apologies.

'I'm sorry. I meant to be back so you'd not have to dish up, but Ryan wants it all done yesterday.'

'Don't worry, everything's gone fine. At least, I've had no complaints so far.'

'There'd better not be, either,' Jeff frowned at the very idea. 'I mean it's bloo-ming good of you to cook for us.'

'Bloo-*ming* good,' Kelly agreed, disjointing the word as he had done—and many of the stockmen before him.

A grin spread over Jeff's face as he realised he was being teased. 'I hope the men have been watching their language, too.'

'Oh, scrupulously. It's been all bloo-mings and da-rns and he-cks. But I think the strain's almost killing them. It's certainly killing me,' she confided with a dry laugh.

Jeff laughed back before saying, 'It's their way of recognising you're a lady.'

'I don't know about that. One of them told his mates I was a "goer",' Kelly relayed, 'which sounds a bit dubious to me.'

'Oh, no, it's a compliment,' Jeff assured. 'It means you're game or plucky—not a whinger.'

'That's nice,' she said quite seriously. 'I was a bit worried they'd think I'm stuck up.'

'Because you're the boss's daughter?'

'No, they didn't seem to know that. More the fact I speak a little differently.'

'You do that,' Jeff confirmed on an admiring note. 'And not just English. Ryan says you speak half a dozen languages.'

'Not quite,' Kelly denied, fluent in only five. 'When did he tell you that?'

'Oh, this morning some time when we were working together. He says you went to a posh finishing school in Switzerland.'

'Really? Tell me, what else did he say?'

'Not much. Only that you weren't likely to stick around for long,' Jeff added with a questioning look.

Distracted, Kelly neither confirmed nor denied the statement. She was too busy puzzling over the reason Ryan had discussed her at all. In her experience, he wasn't given to making idle conversation.

'I think he intended it as a warning,' Jeff added.

'Warning?' Kelly frowned, not following him.

'You know...' the stockman coloured slightly as he explained '...in case I got any ideas about fancying you.'

'Oh, that's absurd!' Kelly exclaimed in annoyance. 'Why should he imagine such a thing? We hardly know each other.'

'I suppose he's being protective towards you,' Jeff suggested.

'*Protective?*' Kelly gave the stockman a scornful look, before realising it wasn't fair to take her anger out on him. She then shook her head to dismiss the subject, and turned back to the stove.

'What about yourself?' he asked when she'd dished up his meal. 'Or would you prefer not to eat with the men?'

'It isn't that. I thought I'd better stay till all the men turn up.'

'There's just Ryan and a couple of labourers to come. Still, if you want to wait and eat in here with him...?'

'Not particularly.' Kelly wrinkled her nose, deciding Ryan's company was something she could do without, and dished up a second plate.

Meals were eaten at a trestle table in the shady part of the camp by the river. As they approached, some of the stockmen shifted along the benches to create a space for them at one end.

Kelly found herself seated opposite MacIver, who welcomed her with a resounding, 'Best grub I've ever had in a mustering camp.'

'Thank you,' she smiled in response.

'Me, too,' a small, wiry man on her right nodded between mouthfuls. 'Haven't tasted food like this since my missus left me.'

'Didn't know you were married, Tom,' one of the younger men commented.

'Wasn't for long,' Tom shrugged. 'A couple of years and she went off back to Brisbane.'

'Couldn't stick the life, I suppose,' MacIver said in a matter-of-fact voice.

'Well, either that or me,' Tom replied and drew a round of laughter from the table.

Kelly laughed too, though she really felt a little sad. Paddy had told her that many of the men had been married at some time, only to be left by their wives within the first year or two. Between the long periods of absence during the mustering season and the claustrophobic closeness of the Wet, it was hard for marriages to survive.

'Takes a special woman to stick it,' was volunteered by the quietly spoken Danny.

'You're right enough, mate,' MacIver agreed as he glanced towards Kelly. 'A goer like the miss here.'

'Mac——' Jeff gave the stockman a warning look, perhaps feeling he had stepped out of line.

But Kelly smiled broadly. 'I'll take that as a compliment, though I'm not sure it's deserved.'

'I reckon it is. Not many women would sign up as a camp cook, for starters,' Mac said to murmurs of agreement.

'To be honest, I haven't signed up exactly,' Kelly said, wondering how best to explain her presence.

'Knowing the boss, he'll have her on trial,' Tom suggested at her hesitant look.

And Kelly had to smile. In a way, the stockman was right. Ryan had her on trial—constantly!

'Well, she gets my vote,' Mac declared, and glanced round to see if anyone was going to give him an argument.

No one did. Hardly surprising when he was built like the side of a house and, though Kelly didn't know it, a champion wrestler in the Territory.

'Jeff'll tell the boss how we feel, won't you?' he said to the head stockman.

Jeff looked less than happy at the request. Like Kelly, he wasn't sure how to explain the real situation. He remembered his own clumsiness when he discovered she was Paddy's daughter and, since arriving at the camp, he'd kept the information to himself.

Still side-stepping it, he replied, ''Fraid not, mate. Kelly was only helping out. She'll be going back to the homestead with Ryan.'

Mac took this news with a disgruntled, 'Should have known it was too bloody good to be true, him hiring a female cook for us.'

'And a pretty one, too,' his friend Tom added.

'So what's happened to Meg Donaldson? Given up on him, has she?' From his tone, Mac obviously didn't have much liking for the Australian woman, and confirmed it by confiding to Kelly, 'Sly bitch, she was. All smiles to the boss, but a face as long as your arm when he wasn't around.'

At this colourful and so accurate description of the housekeeper, Kelly found it impossible to suppress a grin. Mac was obviously a smart character.

It was left to Jeff to make disapproving noises. 'I'd keep your opinions to yourself, mate, if I were you. Meg's still at the homestead, and Ryan won't like you talking about his personal business.'

The criticism drew a grunt from Mac, suggesting he resented it.

But Danny lent his support, saying, 'Ryan's a close one, all right.'

'A good boss, though,' Tom contributed.

'Hard, maybe, but fair,' another man agreed.

'No one was saying different,' Mac piped up again, confiding to Kelly, 'Between him and old Paddy, you won't find a better boss in the Territory... Still, you'll have met his dad if you're working at the homestead.'

Kelly nodded and realised it was time to own up.

However, before she could, Mac ran on, 'They're not much alike, mind you, though maybe that's understandable with Ryan being adopted.'

'*MacIver!*' Jeff almost barked at the stockman, his earlier lecture having clearly been forgotten.

Mac went on the defensive, muttering, 'I'm not saying nothing everyone doesn't know. Unless it's news to the miss here...?'

'No, I knew,' Kelly admitted.

'There you are, then,' Mac directed at the head stockman, feeling he'd been vindicated.

Frustrated, Jeff looked to Kelly in apology, blaming himself for the increasingly awkward situation. Kelly, however, considered it her fault and, before Mac could blunder on further, she decided to make a plain statement.

'The truth is, Mac, I'm not really working at the homestead. You see, Paddy... well, he's my——' She faltered once, then broke off mid-sentence.

For there, at the head of the table, stood Ryan, his appearance so sudden the words went clean out of her head. She forgot even the gist of what she'd been saying, as her eyes met his and everyone else seemed to just fade away.

CHAPTER EIGHT

IT WAS the same for Ryan. He approached almost unnoticed, and took in the situation at a glance. Then his
eyes went from the circle of male faces to the girl who
so effortlessly held their attention.

He wondered why he should be surprised, why he
expected his men to be any different. Even he'd recognised that she had charm. It didn't just lie in her looks
but in odd things, like the way she would suddenly smile.
He'd watched that charm work on every man who came
near her, and thought himself immune because he could
see right through her.

Yet there were times when it made no difference. Times
when he'd come upon her, as now, and realise all over
again how beautiful she was. Times when she'd stare at
him with those wide green eyes until a knife seemed to
twist inside him. It was then he took refuge in anger,
knowing he couldn't let himself feel anything else. Not
for this girl. Not when she was Paddy's little princess—
however false the image.

But more than that stopped him, Ryan admitted as he
returned her stare. He also knew that one day she was
going to get up and go. It was inevitable as the rains in
November, and he had no intention of being part of the
wreckage she left behind.

The thought alone brought a scowl to his face, which,
in turn, snapped Kelly out of her daze. She wondered
what she'd done wrong now, but could hardly ask. Some
of the men were already eyeing Ryan and her curiously,
the silence between them telling.

It was finally broken by Tom saying, 'Sit here, boss,'
as he shifted up the bench to create a space between Kelly
and himself.

Ryan hesitated so long, Kelly thought he might actually refuse, but eventually he came round the table to sit down with his meal. He'd helped himself to a generous portion of stew and, along with some of the stockmen, she waited for his verdict.

He was three-quarters finished when he raised his head to find several pairs of eyes on him. 'Something wrong?'

'No, boss,' Mac answered for them all. 'We were just wondering what you thought of the miss's grub.'

'Well,' Ryan slid a wry, sideways glance at Kelly before volunteering, 'I've tasted worse.'

Hardly complimentary, she thought as she retorted, 'You don't *have* to eat it, you know!'

'No, but I'll be polite,' he had the nerve to say and, resuming his meal, missed the murderous look she gave him.

It was Jeff who felt the need to put in, 'Ryan's just joking.'

'Course he is,' Mac seconded. 'Aren't you, boss?'

'Probably,' Ryan smiled as he pushed aside a now empty plate.

But Kelly's face remained stony. Compliments she hadn't expected. A little gratitude, however, wouldn't have killed him.

'A pity the miss isn't staying,' Mac went on. 'A decent cook like her, and I might work for half-pay.'

'Me, too,' Tom echoed the sentiment.

And, while Kelly blushed slightly, Ryan remarked in amused tones, 'Sounds like you could save me a fortune. The question is—could I afford you?'

'That depends,' she played along. 'What's the job pay?'

'Well, I reckon I could offer you top rate, what with the saving I'd make on Mac's and Tom's.'

Now it was the stockmen's turn to look doubtful, wondering whether Ryan was joking or not. For they still didn't know who Kelly was.

'Don't worry, it'll never happen,' Jeff assured them. 'A girl like Kelly isn't going to waste her time cooking for a bunch like you.'

'Suppose not,' Tom conceded without taking offence.

And Mac sighed, 'Then we'll just have to put up with Christy—God help us.'

Remembering Christy's fate, Kelly waited to see if Ryan or Jeff would say anything.

It was Ryan who stated flatly, 'No, you won't. I've sacked him.'

There was a moment's silence and an exchange of glances between the stockmen, before Danny said, 'Don't blame you, boss.'

It drew a general murmur of agreement, and some comments that suggested the absent Christy wasn't the most popular character around.

'Hopefully Davidson will find someone better in Katherine,' Jeff added.

'Not going to be as good as the miss here, though,' grumbled Mac, who'd clearly become Kelly's biggest fan.

Tom wasn't far behind, echoing, 'Too true.'

'Not as pretty either, I imagine,' Ryan suggested drily, well aware it wasn't entirely Kelly's cooking skills that had won them over.

'You said it, boss!' Mac confirmed with a grin. 'We can see why you'd want to keep her on the homestead.'

The stockman cast Kelly an admiring glance, but she was oblivious, her own eyes fixed on Ryan. Had he actually called her pretty? She couldn't remember him ever noticing her looks before.

For a moment she felt inordinately pleased, then he made a point of denying any personal interest in her.

'It's not me but Paddy who'd give you the argument.'

'Paddy?'

Clearly the stockman didn't understand, and Ryan looked at Kelly, his eyes questioning how much she'd revealed. She shook her head and, with a helpless look, tried to convey how difficult it had been.

But he made it seem simple as he turned back to Mac to coolly remark, 'You obviously haven't realised—Paddy is Kelly's father.'

A silence followed while his words sank in, and Kelly stared at him, astonished by his frankness.

'Paddy's her father,' Mac eventually repeated, his booming tones travelling down to the far end of the table and making poor Kelly wish the ground would just swallow her up. 'Well, stone me! Paddy's daughter—and there's me, stupid enough to think you were the new cook.'

'It's my fault, really,' Kelly said in fairness. 'I should have told you earlier.'

But Jeff muttered, 'You hardly got the chance,' with an accusing look at the stockman.

And he conceded, 'Aye, me and my big mouth.'

'We must have been blind, too,' Tom put in, 'for you're the spit of Paddy. Isn't she, Danny?'

Danny nodded. 'Only prettier,' he said, with a gentle gallantry that made Kelly smile.

Then the irrepressible Mac came back with, 'You know, the funny thing is I didn't even know Paddy had a daughter.'

'No, well...' Ryan paused briefly to select an excuse, 'Kelly's mother wanted her to be brought up and educated in Europe rather than Australia.'

Kelly had to admit it was clever. Without telling any real lies, it gave quite the wrong impression.

From the general nodding, it satisfied the men, though Tom added, 'Didn't even know Paddy had been married a second time.'

Kelly felt a betraying blush hit her cheeks and she looked to Ryan, waiting for him to set the record straight. But he just looked back at her, raising his brows in a 'does-it-matter?' gesture. So she followed his lead and let Tom's assumption go. It seemed preferable to embarrassing everybody with the truth.

In any event, lunch time was over, the stockmen already beginning to rise from the table until there was just Jeff, enjoying a more exclusive share of Kelly's company, and Ryan, very much aware of the fact.

'You'd better go and check the hessian's secure,' he finally instructed.

'OK.' The head stockman took the hint and departed with a smiling, 'See you later,' to Kelly.

Finding herself alone with Ryan, she too rose to start collecting the dirty plates.

He stood with her. 'You don't have to do that.'

'I don't mind.' She continued along the table, hoping he might go away if she ignored him.

Instead, to her amazement, he began helping her to clear away. When they met at the last dish, he took the whole pile from her hands. The metal plates were heavy, though most had been scraped clean.

'Don't look as if they'll need much washing,' he commented, smiling slightly.

'No,' she agreed, but her tone was stiff in comparison.

'I suppose I should thank you,' he added as they walked towards the cook-house trailer.

It sounded grudging to Kelly, and she muttered, 'Don't force yourself,' before stalking ahead of him.

With a sigh of exasperation, Ryan followed her up the steps to deposit the plates in the sink.

'All right,' he tried again, 'I underestimated you. If your stew's anything to go by, you're a pretty good cook.'

It still sounded an effort for him to admit that much, but Kelly unbent a fraction to remark, 'As long as the men enjoyed it.'

'No doubt about that. You seem to have made a big hit with them,' Ryan said in a speculative tone.

'They're a nice bunch,' Kelly replied absently, more intent on pumping water into a kettle.

Ryan waited until she'd placed it on the stove before asking, 'What about Jeff?'

This time he was awarded a long, considering stare, followed by an obstructive, 'What about Jeff?'

'Do you like him?' he pursued, regardless.

However, Kelly proved she was well ahead of him. 'Yes, I like him. No, I don't fancy him. Neither am I likely to... Does that about cover it?'

'OK, I was being obvious,' Ryan admitted, smiling in spite of himself. 'But, to be honest, I'm more worried about Jeff's susceptibility. There's few enough women round here, and none with your sort of looks.'

'Really?' Kelly wasn't sure how to take this. From any other man it would be a flattering remark, but somehow he made it seem an accusation.

'At any rate,' he continued, 'I'd be grateful if you discouraged him.'

For a moment Kelly looked at him in disbelief, then almost laughed as the irony of the situation struck her. There was Jeff, thinking Ryan was concerned about her. And instead it was the stockman he was trying to protect—presumably from her bad influence.

'Oh, and how am I meant to do that?' she finally enquired.

He shrugged, then suggested drily, 'You could always talk to him the way you do me. That should work.'

Kelly pulled a face. '*You're* hardly all sunshine and light yourself, you know.'

'Possibly not,' Ryan conceded. 'We seem to bring out the worst in each other. But maybe if we tried a little harder to get on...' He trailed off, leaving the next move to her.

Suspicious that he'd even made the first one, Kelly said hesitantly, 'Well, yes... we could try.'

'Only you don't think we'd succeed,' he concluded from her tone.

She shook her head. 'Not really, no.'

Yet for once there was no hostility in the exchange. Just an acceptance that some things would always stand between them.

They stared at each other in silence for a moment, before their peace was shattered by a roaring noise overhead.

'That's the choppers,' Ryan said as Kelly jerked her head upwards.

'Choppers? You mean *helicopters*?' she asked, though the whirring sound was distinct enough.

He nodded. 'We hire them to help with bigger mustering operations. Come and have a look.'

They climbed out of the trailer in time to catch sight of two helicopters flying over the stockyards.

'This may seem terribly ignorant,' Kelly said, 'but what do you actually use them for? Surely you don't collect the cattle in them?'

'Not quite.' Ryan looked amused at the idea. 'If you like, you can come up in the Cessna with me—watch them in action.'

Tempted, Kelly said conscientiously, 'What about the dishes?'

Ryan waved the objection aside. 'Leave them for the new cook.'

'OK.' She didn't need any more persuading and, switching off the stove, fell in step beside him.

They walked towards the yards first and found Jeff saddling up a couple of horses. He smiled at Kelly, with no more than pleasantness, she thought. But Ryan obviously thought differently, his voice abrupt as he asked, 'Everything ready?'

Jeff nodded. 'I think so. The men have already ridden out, and Hyland's just arrived with the choppers... I've also picked out a quiet horse for Kelly, if she wants to watch the mustering,' he added, sending her another smile.

'Well, that's kind of you——' About to make a perfectly valid excuse, Kelly was cut off mid-sentence.

'She's going up in the Cessna with me,' Ryan announced, again in an abrupt tone.

This time it was noticed by the stockman who flushed as he mumbled, 'Yes, of course.'

'You'd better catch up with the men,' Ryan suggested coolly, before taking Kelly's arm and leading her towards one of the jeeps.

'Still think it's my imagination?' he asked when they'd climbed in.

'If you mean about Jeff—yes, I do,' Kelly replied, ignoring any doubts she might have. 'There was certainly no need to cut me off like that. I was going to refuse, you know.'

'Possibly.'

'*Definitely!* Would you like to know why?'

'I have a feeling you're going to tell me, anyway.'

He was right as Kelly haughtily informed him, 'I was hardly likely to accept, considering I can't even ride.'

'You can't ride?' Ryan's brows shot up. 'Are you serious? You really can't ride?'

'No, *I really can't ride*,' she mimicked his incredulous tone. 'Whereas I suppose you could, practically from the day you learned to walk.'

'Practically,' Ryan echoed, laughing despite her frosty expression, and turning away to start the jeep.

'You're not scared of horses, are you?' he added as they drove towards the Cessna.

'No, of course not!' Kelly was suitably indignant.

'OK, I was just asking,' he sighed at her touchiness. 'Recalling your exploits on a motorbike, I should have known better. So why can't you ride?'

Kelly shrugged. 'I've never felt the need to learn.'

'No, I don't suppose it's a necessary social asset in your circles,' he said in a dry voice. 'So what did that fancy finishing school teach you?'

'Some German, French, Italian, deportment, *haute cuisine* ... oh, and how to catch a rich husband,' Kelly added out of sheer devilment.

As expected, he took her seriously. 'Well, the last certainly won't be much good to you out here. Not that

you'd ever consider settling in the Outback, would you?'
he said, glancing momentarily from the road.

Assuming it was a rhetorical question, Kelly didn't
bother replying. She knew there was no home for her
here. He'd made that plain from the beginning, so what
could he expect her to say? Yet it seemed he'd expected
something, for he frowned at her silence.

By then they'd reached the clearing to find the helicopters had landed on either side of the plane. The pilot
of one came to greet them, shaking Ryan's hand as he
said, 'I heard you'd returned. So how was France?'

'Very French,' Ryan replied with a slight grimace.

Whatever he took the comment to mean, the man
laughed before his eyes switched to Kelly. 'Still, you seem
to have brought back a very pretty souvenir.'

Kelly accepted the compliment with a shy smile, while
the pilot waited for an introduction from Ryan.

It was brief to the point of rudeness. 'Kelly
Cormack...Jim Hyland.'

'Mr Hyland.' Politely Kelly extended a hand.

'Miss Cormack.' The man shook it, offering her a grin.
'With a name like that, you must be Irish.'

'Well, my folks were—both of them,' she responded,
then slid a sideways glance at Ryan.

Perhaps he took it as a threat to reveal her parentage,
for he quickly curtailed the conversation, saying, 'Jim
and I have some business to discuss. Why don't you wait
in the plane? It'll be cooler there.'

'How thoughtful of you,' she said with acid sweetness,
and walked off towards the plane.

It was no cooler than on the ground. Stationary and
with the doors off, it was scarcely likely to be. She was
almost relieved when Ryan joined her, though she gave
no sign of it as they sat in silence, waiting for the
helicopters to take off first.

Their whirring blades sent up a cloud of red-grey dust,
and the roar of the engines was near deafening as they
lifted vertically into the air. The Cessna, of course,

needed to taxi the length of the clearing before take-off, but this time Kelly felt no nervousness. The journey here had proved Ryan was competent at handling the light aircraft.

As they flew over the stockyards, she saw that a new construction had been erected since the morning. It looked like sacking, two high walls of it running from the mouth of the mustering yards for about seven hundred yards to fan out to roughly the same distance across.

'What's that for?' she asked, any anger forgotten.

'The hessian, you mean?'

'Yes, I think so.'

'It acts as a funnel. The idea is to drive the cattle round the side of the hill, so they'll run blind between the two walls. Then it's just a matter of channelling them into the yards.'

Ryan made it sound simple, but Kelly was still rather hazy about the function of the aircraft in this operation.

At first they passed over the herd grazing by the river, and flew to where the stockmen had gathered. The helicopters were also hovering overhead, waiting for Ryan to appear, and as he circled the Cessna back towards the cattle the two pilots rose to fly in formation.

At their approach the cattle started to shift ground. Realising it was the drone of the engines that was going to be used to drive them in the desired direction, Kelly remained puzzled as to how this could be done without causing a stampede.

It turned out to be a matter of patience, timing and skilful flying. Instead of swooping down on the herd, they dropped by degrees, lower and lower, the choppers hovering, the Cessna continually banking, circling and returning. It was all done very gradually so that the cattle began moving in a mob, following the contours of the land towards the hill, while the stockmen rode in at their tail. Then they increased the pressure, dropping down until they were flying barely twenty feet from the ground, in a tremendous cloud of dust and roar of sound.

Between the aircraft noise and the calls, whistles and whip-cracking of the stockmen, the protesting steers were urged round the hill to flow, unawares, into the trap laid for them. The two walls of hessian flapped madly in the wind created by the choppers, yet, for all their apparent flimsiness, the cattle made no attempt to break through these artificial barriers, and instead streamed into the stockyards, where the rest of the men were waiting for them.

Apart from coughing back the dust, Kelly sat through it all in absolute silence. But her eyes grew wider by the second, uncertain whether to be fascinated or just plain terrified. It seemed a miracle, among this confusion of dust and sound, that they hadn't crashed into the ground or into one of the choppers, barely a wing span apart. Yet when she glanced from time to time at Ryan, his expression was superbly cool, as if he didn't even recognise such a possibility.

Soon the main herd was mustered in the yards, and the aircraft circled back to pick up some of the young steers that had managed to break away. This operation seemed hardly less dangerous, as they flew just above the level of the high grass, flushing the cattle out of hiding and driving them towards the bull catchers, who had the strenuous task of rolling the beast over and holding it down long enough to strap the hind legs.

The first time Kelly watched this being done, it was by the huge, heavily muscled Mac, and she thought it must just be a matter of brute strength. But later she saw the same operation being performed by his friend Tom who, with his small, wiry frame, had to rely on surprise, speed and agility to rope the fierce-looking bulls. What struck her the most, however, was the way both men came out of the fray, grinning from ear to ear. Hard and dirty and dangerous the work might be, but there was nothing else they'd rather do.

She gained the same impression from Ryan. Gone was the unsociable loner of the Hotel Arbois, the impatient traveller on the journey home. This was his element and, in it, he exuded confidence and strength. If the irreverent stockmen called him boss, it had to be because he'd earned the title. And that afternoon, sitting beside him as he proved himself a magnificent flyer, even Kelly could appreciate some of the reasons.

By the time they finally landed back in the clearing, she'd long lost any sense of nervousness. In fact, she'd begun to wish that she could fly, too. It was a breathtaking experience.

'Are you OK?' Ryan asked, when he switched off the engine and turned to catch her far-away look.

'Oh, yes, fine,' she replied, coming back to earth.

'Just that you've hardly said a word all afternoon,' he pointed out.

Kelly was surprised he'd noticed. 'I was scared I'd distract you.'

'You're probably right. In fact, maybe I shouldn't have taken you up at all.'

'Oh.' Kelly felt curiously hurt.

'I mean, between the dust and the noise, it couldn't have been much of a picnic for you,' he continued, making her realise he was actually apologising.

She brightened considerably. 'No, I enjoyed it. Really, I did. I was just thinking I wouldn't mind learning to fly myself.'

The idea took Ryan aback and he looked less than enthusiastic. 'I don't know. It might be better if you learned how to ride first.'

'For better read safer?' Kelly challenged, sure he was thinking of her bike accident.

'Perhaps,' he admitted in a wry tone, then tacking on, 'Certainly more useful if you were sticking around for a while...'

A steady stare turned the comment into a question— a question which totally threw Kelly. Surely he wanted her gone as soon as possible? Yet the way he was looking at her, an odd intentness in his eyes, seemed to suggest otherwise. And for a moment she had a crazy urge to tell him she'd stick around—stick around just as long he asked her to.

Crazy, she repeated to herself and, suppressing the urge, murmured, 'I suppose so.' She thought it sounded vague and non-committal.

But apparently not to Ryan, who ran on, 'Then I'll pick out a horse when we get back. There's a bay that might suit you—nice temperament and only fourteen hands.'

'Well, as long as it's got four feet,' Kelly joked at her own ignorance on horsy matters.

He laughed in response, a deep, attractive laugh, and Kelly wondered if there wasn't hope for them yet. Maybe with a little effort they could become friends.

His indulgent mood continued as they drove back to the stockyards, and he kept her at his side for most of the afternoon while he supervised the selecting and branding of the cattle. He seemed not to mind the men's half teasing, half admiring attitude to her.

When she heard a 'train' would be coming the next day to transport the cattle to Katherine, Kelly asked in all innocence, 'Is there a rail station nearby?'

It drew a general round of laughter before Ryan took pity on her, explaining, 'Danny was referring to what we call a "road train". That's a series of self-tracking trailers.'

'Oh.' Kelly nodded intelligently and waited until the men were busy again to ask, 'What's a self-tracking trailer when it's at home?'

With an amused glance, Ryan confided, 'What you'd probably call a container lorry, only several strung together and pulled by the same diesel truck.'

'It must be pretty big to take all these cattle.' Kelly surveyed the now teeming mustering yards.

Ryan agreed, 'Yes, it's some sight, thundering along the Highway.'

'The Track, you mean,' Kelly put in, showing she remembered their name for the local highway.

'Right.' He awarded her an approving smile. 'We'll have you educated yet.'

'And there was me thinking I had been,' she returned drily.

'In some things, maybe,' he granted. 'Just not what counts out here.'

Kelly accepted the truth of that, laughing in response, 'Well, how was I to know this would be my destiny?'

She clearly meant it as a joke, looking askance at the stamping, snorting steers, and making a play of choking on the dust-storm they were creating.

Ryan laughed too at first, then confused her by asking, 'Is it?'

'Is it what?'

'Your destiny?'

There was no humour in the question, no humour in Ryan's expression, either. Kelly recognised that as she glanced at his rigidly handsome profile. And, though his eyes were fixed on the branding, she sensed him waiting for an answer.

It was the second time that day he'd virtually asked her how long she would be staying. The answer was obviously important to him. But why?

She supposed Kilconnell Downs must be the issue. He still imagined she had designs on his precious station. The idea hurt.

'Come on, can you really see me, "Home on the range, where the deer and the kangaroo play"?' she misquoted on a flippant note.

It was surely what he wanted to hear, yet he didn't look pleased. In fact, after giving her a brief, hard stare, he slipped down from the railing where they were seated and went to take over from Danny.

As she watched him hold down the steers to be branded, Kelly suspected the poor cattle were being punished for something she'd done. She just didn't know what.

Fortunately the work put him back in a better temper by the time dusk fell. They'd stayed longer than he'd intended and, because they were returning by road, a journey of some hours, he suggested they have supper at the camp.

A new cook had arrived late in the afternoon, an Italian who'd worked in a Darwin restaurant before it had gone out of business. For his debut he made a beef casserole, richly flavoured, and, in Kelly's opinion, superior to her own efforts at lunch. But the men didn't appear to agree, grumbling that the sauce tasted queer and loyally declaring her the better cook.

Kelly didn't take all this flattery too seriously. She was just pleased they seemed to like her, an impression reinforced when she finally climbed into an old pick-up truck with Ryan and the men gathered round to wave them off.

'Well, I never knew I was so popular,' Ryan commented on the chorus of farewells as they drew away.

If Kelly recognised the irony, she chose to ignore it. The day had proved largely enjoyable, and she didn't want to spoil it by quarrelling.

Instead she leaned her head back against the seat and, despite the bumping and rattling of the aged truck, soon fell fast asleep. She must have been exhausted because she didn't wake when her head slipped downwards to rest on Ryan's shoulder. Nor did she stir as he lifted his arm, allowing her to burrow against his chest before settling on his lap.

When finally she did open her eyes, Kelly was very disorientated. The truck was no longer in motion, and it took her several seconds to remember where she'd fallen asleep; then another several to realise that, somewhere along the way, she'd decided to spread herself out on the truck's bench seat.

But she didn't immediately pull away. She couldn't really, as an arm held her while a hand stroked her hair. For a moment Kelly thought it was her imagination, that light, caressing touch. So gentle, she couldn't believe it came from Ryan or was meant for her.

Only she had to, as the hand went on stroking, smoothing back the curls from her face, occasionally brushing against her cheek, until her heart turned over with a feeling she didn't even want to name.

Then suddenly he stopped, his hand moving to her shoulder to shake her from sleep. No longer gentle, he was almost rough as he said, 'Come on, Kelly, wake up. We're here.'

At this reversion to normal, Kelly's pride also returned. She went through a pretence of coming awake and quickly sat away from him. For his voice alone convinced her she'd been right all the time. The affection wasn't for her. He'd simply forgotten who she was, just as he had once before.

'Sorry, must have been tired,' she mumbled, leaving him to read it as an excuse for dumping herself on him in the first place.

'That's OK. It's been a long day,' he replied less abruptly and, climbing down from the truck, went round to open her door.

Kelly beat him to it, an act of independence subsequently ruined by her stumbling out of the pick-up. She might actually have fallen if he hadn't placed a supportive hand on her arm.

'Circulation gone?' he asked.

'A little.' She stamped her foot experimentally and uttered a pained, 'Ouch,' as pins and needles attacked her leg.

'Maybe I'd better carry you,' he suggested.

'No, thank you,' Kelly responded hastily, and began walking, however stiffly, up the pathway to the bungalow.

All the lights were out, Paddy long since gone to bed, and they padded quietly along the corridor.

They came to Ryan's room first and Kelly whispered, ''Night, then.'

But when she would have walked away, he caught her arm. 'Kelly, listen——'

'Yes?' She looked at him in expectation.

However, it seemed he changed his mind about what he wanted to say, for he simply added, 'See you tomorrow.'

'Yes, see you,' she echoed, with an odd sense of let-down, then continued on to her room.

But, as she undressed for bed, Kelly wondered if he'd meant anything more. After all, living in the same house, it was inevitable they'd see each other tomorrow. So maybe it had really been a form of unspoken understanding—that when tomorrow came they'd still be friends.

She shook her head, dismissing the idea as fanciful. One day couldn't turn everything round. Nothing had made him stop believing all those lies about her and, until he did, they'd never be friends—or anything more.

Yet later, as Kelly drifted off to sleep, she still imagined a gentle hand stroking her hair.

CHAPTER NINE

KELLY rose late the next morning to find Paddy waiting for her on the front porch. He wanted to hear all about her day out, so she began by giving him her impressions of the flight to the camp and the Outback scenery, then she told him of her temporary appointment as camp cook, relaying some of the men's more comic remarks, and finally she described the excitement of the actual mustering operation. Altogether she managed to give an entire account of her day, without mentioning Ryan's name once.

A curious Paddy had to ask for himself, 'And how did the two of you get on?'

'Oh, you know,' she shrugged with studied casualness.

'Now, Kelly girl, would I be asking if I knew?'

'All right—so-so.'

'So-so?' Paddy weighed this totally uninformative phrase, before adding in his gently teasing brogue, 'Sure now, doesn't that tell me a lot? Almost as much as the man himself.'

'Ryan...what did he say?' Again Kelly pretended only casual interest.

'Well, as I recall, it was quite complimentary.' Paddy smiled at the memory.

He seemed in no hurry, however, to share it with Kelly, instead leaving her curiosity to dangle until she was forced to ask a second time, 'So what *did* he say?'

'Oh, that you didn't get in the way too much,' Paddy relayed, 'and that at least you weren't a whinger.'

'*That's* complimentary?' Kelly couldn't see it.

'In Ryan's book, it would be,' Paddy assured with a small chuckle.

But Kelly didn't feel particularly complimented. She hadn't been a nuisance or a whinger. Big deal!

'You can ask him, if you like,' Paddy suggested. 'It seems he'll be joining us for lunch. So I heard him telling Meg, anyway.'

'That should please her,' Kelly said in an almost sour tone.

And Paddy wisely deemed it time to change the subject, although he suspected that pleasing Meg Donaldson wasn't in his son's mind at all.

Unfathomable! That was Kelly's verdict when later she sat opposite Ryan. He'd reverted to being his usual *un*talkative self, and she followed suit. But more often than not, when she glanced up from the table, it was to find him staring at her, until she began to feel like one of the cattle being judged for auction.

Then suddenly, at the very end of the meal, he announced, 'About those riding lessons—we can start this afternoon if you want.'

It was so unexpected that she could only gape at him in return. Yesterday, when he'd suggested she should learn, she had scarcely imagined he'd been volunteering himself as a teacher. She scarcely believed it now.

'That's a fine idea, son,' Paddy said, making up for her lack of response. 'You'll have picked out a horse, will you?'

'That two-year-old bay, sired by Waterford,' Ryan said shortly.

And Paddy nodded in approval. 'Sure, he's a good-tempered beast.'

But it went unnoticed, as Ryan's eyes switched back to Kelly, in time to see her surprised look turn into a frown. He imagined her desperately searching for an excuse—any excuse so long as she didn't have to be with him.

Angered, he deliberately thwarted her by saying, 'I'll meet you at the tack shed at four,' and rose to go back to work before she had the chance to refuse.

Paddy was left beaming in satisfaction. 'Now, isn't that grand of him?'

'Oh, grand,' Kelly echoed sceptically.

Just as she'd been too shocked to turn down Ryan's offer, she had a feeling he'd had his arm twisted to make it. Gently and amiably, knowing Paddy's methods, but twisted all the same.

And when the hour came it was with the same gentleness that he reminded her of the four o'clock appointment she'd been trying conveniently to forget.

She arrived at the tack-room ten minutes late, to find Ryan already there. He greeted her with an abrupt, 'Thought you weren't coming.'

Wishful thinking? she almost asked him, but confined herself to shrugging, 'I forgot the time.'

Unimpressed by the excuse, Ryan handed her some bridle equipment to carry, before slinging a saddle over his arm. Then, without another word, he walked out off the tack-room and headed towards the yards.

Kelly assumed she was meant to trail after him. 'Look, I'm sorry if Paddy forced you into this,' she said, more resentful than apologetic as she half ran to keep up with him.

He broke stride for a moment to award her a slight scowl, before admitting stiffly, 'He didn't. It was my idea.'

'Oh!' she murmured in surprise.

'I thought you should learn to ride while you're here, but if you don't want to——' He shrugged and made to turn back in the direction they'd come.

'It isn't that!' she said, hastily blocking his path. 'I do want to learn, really. I just don't want it to be under any sufferance on your part. You know what I mean?'

'Vaguely.' Ryan nodded at her rather garbled explanation. 'However, I don't think you have to worry about me. After all, as the instructor, I doubt *I'll* be the one doing the *suffering*,' he pointed out.

Kelly didn't quite catch on until his mouth slanted with amusement. Then she pulled a face at what she assumed was his little joke. At least, she hoped it was, as he added, 'Still, we'll take it nice and easy.' And, with a smile, he waited for her to fall in step beside him again.

Eventually they reached a pen at the far end of the homestead, well away from cattle or activity of any kind. In the pen was a horse, light brown in colour with a darker, flowing mane.

It was love at first sight for Kelly as she sat on the top rail and watched the horse 'showing off' by friskily circling the pen a couple of times before approaching at Ryan's whistle.

'God, he's beautiful.' Her tone was almost one of awe as she climbed down from the fence to stand a cautious yard away.

'Yes—unfortunately he knows it,' Ryan laughed wryly while he stroked the nose playfully butting his chest.

'Is it OK if I touch him?' Kelly asked, not yet daring to.

'Sure. Come and be introduced.' Ryan recognised her nervousness and, taking her arm, gently drew her closer. 'Enniscorthy—this is your new owner. Kelly Cormack, this is Enniscorthy.'

'Enniscorthy,' she repeated, still with a hint of awe.

'Rather a mouthful of a name, I'm afraid,' Ryan went on. 'Paddy had this tradition of calling the horses after Irish place names, only we've run out of the shorter variety.'

'Oh, I think it suits him,' Kelly smiled, already making friends with the bay as she held out a sugar lump brought precisely for that purpose.

Ryan noted the action with a wry, 'Well, I can see he's going to be the most spoilt animal on the station.'

'Is he really mine?' Kelly wondered if his 'owner' had just been a manner of speech.

But he nodded, 'Provided you look after him properly, of course.'

'Oh, I will,' she promised eagerly, altogether forgetting how little time she'd be around to do so, and once more Ryan found himself puzzled by her.

Earlier, at lunch, she'd been all cool superiority, so unapproachable that he had waited the entire meal to suggest the riding lessons, and felt a bloody fool in doing so. Now, with those big green eyes trained on him, she looked almost painfully young, and he felt——

'What's wrong?' she asked, making him realise he'd been staring.

He shook his head and dismissed his thoughts with an impatient frown. 'Let's get started.'

Sobered by his brusqueness, Kelly handed him the tackle she'd been carrying.

'Watch carefully.' He showed her how to put the bit between the horse's teeth and loop the halter over his neck, cautioning her on possible errors. Then he reversed his actions, leaving her to try it.

Kelly approached the task with some nervousness but, if Enniscorthy was aware of it, he politely put up with her efforts, and she managed to do it right first time.

Unfortunately, she had less success with the saddle. She thought she copied Ryan's instructions to the letter, until he tugged at a stirrup and the whole thing slipped to one side.

'I can't understand it,' she said, watching as he repositioned it. 'What did I get wrong?'

'Nothing, I suspect,' Ryan smiled slightly. 'Enniscorthy's just played a little trick on you. While you were tightening the girth strap, he blew out his stomach, so that with it back to normal the saddle was bound to slide.'

'Oh.' Kelly looked askance at the bay, wondering if he had any more smart tricks planned for her.

When Ryan said, 'Ready to mount?' she wasn't so sure.

'He is broken in, isn't he?' she asked, stalling for time.

'Fully,' he claimed wryly. 'So come on. We'll do it the easy way. You grip the saddle horn and use my hands as a stirrup. Then, when I give you a boost, pull yourself up and try and swing your other leg over. Right?'

'Right,' Kelly echoed rather weakly and, after a hefty boost from Ryan, succeeded in swinging her leg over the saddle—only to almost fall off the other side.

Luckily, Ryan straightened in time to save her by bracing a hand against her thigh. 'Don't worry. I won't let you get hurt,' he said at her visibly shaken reaction.

It seemed an odd promise for him to make, but Kelly still felt reassured, if a little self-conscious, as she mumbled back, 'I'm fine now.'

He nodded and, removing his hand, attached a leading rein to the bridle. 'First we'll walk up and down the pen a few times, but don't bother with the reins. Just sit straight, and try and get a sense of balance.'

'All right.' Kelly was quite happy to do as instructed. She held on to the pommel of the saddle, kept her feet firmly tucked in the stirrups, and let Ryan and Enniscorthy do the rest.

For a couple of turns of the enclosure he remained at the horse's head, before gradually extending the leading rein to full stretch. Then he took up stance in the middle of the pen, while a well-trained Enniscorthy circled him at a walking pace.

Kelly thought she was doing rather well—even if she was doing very little—but after some minutes' appraisal, Ryan disillusioned her.

'Straighten your back!' he called out. 'You're sitting there like a sack of potatoes.'

'All right,' Kelly muttered, doing as ordered, but not without a resentful glare.

'And lift up your head,' he said next.

'Why?'

'Because you should keep your eyes in front of you, not fixed on the horse.'

Kelly didn't see the logic of that. 'But if I don't watch the horse, how do I know what he's doing?' she argued.

Ryan looked heavenward, before saying with heavy patience, 'At present, I think you can safely assume he'll keep walking in a circle, unless I tell him differently. In the future, I'd hope he'll do what *you* tell him. Either way, you don't have to constantly watch him. OK?'

'OK!' Kelly retorted, fuming at this little lecture, though she did lift her head to stare rigidly ahead.

It took another couple of turns for her to trust that Enniscorthy really wasn't going to make any sudden moves, but she eventually began to gain a shade more confidence.

Only to have Ryan say, 'You're slouching again.'

Kelly exploded. 'I am not slouching! I *never* slouch! If I was taught anything at that bloody finishing school, it was good posture,' she claimed indignantly.

Ryan couldn't fail to notice he'd touched a nerve but, despite the eyes flashing angrily at him, his mouth curved into a smile.

Seeing it, Kelly realised her reaction had been a little excessive. 'All right, perhaps I was leaning forwards slightly. But that's how I've seen people riding in films.'

'Yes, well...what people do in films seldom bears any relation to real life,' Ryan said very drily. 'Or haven't you discovered that yet?'

'I'm beginning to.' Kelly pulled a slight face in return.

'The point is—do you want to learn properly or not?' he added.

'I suppose so,' she said in grudging tones.

'Well, that means doing what you're told. A new experience for you, I realise,' he said with a wry look, 'so I'll make a few concessions.'

'Like what?' Kelly enquired suspiciously as he came to stand at her side.

'Oh, like putting up with a certain number of your smart remarks,' he drawled. 'Provided you at least try and obey any instructions I give you ... Is it a deal?'

Though he smiled up at her, Kelly still felt wary. And for a moment she was tempted to say something hard and careless, something that would keep their distance, wide and safe. No playing at an ambiguous friendship, no getting hurt...

But in the end she echoed quietly, 'A deal, yes.'

'Good.' Ryan nodded in approval, then he added, 'For now, I think we'd better call it a day.'

'But I've hardly learned anything,' Kelly said, disappointed.

'You will. It's just not a good idea to spend too long in the saddle on your first day. Not if you want to be able to sit down the second, anyway,' he pointed out. 'But you can stay on, while I lead Enniscorthy back to his stable.'

'No, it's all right. I'll get down now.' Kelly preferred no witnesses to her helplessness.

'All right, swing your leg over till you're sitting on the saddle,' Ryan instructed.

She did so quite easily, but then looked doubtfully down at the ground. 'You'll have to move if I'm going to jump.'

'You're not!' Ryan gave her one of his more usual looks of exasperation before reaching up to put his hands on her waist.

By the time Kelly realised his intention, he was already lifting her from the saddle. He landed her safely enough, then held on to her until she could find her balance. It was only for a moment, but when she swayed against him Kelly felt an acute awareness of Ryan as a man. She almost jumped away, a clumsy move that had her knocking back into Enniscorthy.

The horse protested by shifting a few paces and giving a small whinny of complaint. He was pacified by Ryan stroking his mane with a dry comment of, 'Don't worry, boy. It's me she reckons has the infectious disease.'

'It's not that. It's just...' Kelly faltered, blushing furiously.

'Forget it,' Ryan eventually said, letting her off the hook. 'I know it's my fault—the way I've acted in the past... But you don't need to be nervous now, OK?' he finished on a serious note.

'OK.' Kelly gave a shy nod in return.

Then he said, friendly again, 'Here, you take Enniscorthy.'

He handed her the leading rein while he went to open the gate. She tugged gently on it, and was surprised when Enniscorthy actually began following her. She smiled at the idea that maybe he knew he was *her* horse now.

They walked back to the stable block, behind the main stockyards, and Ryan showed her where to stall him.

'I'll return this gear for you,' he said, picking up the bridle and saddle. 'How about another lesson—same time tomorrow?'

'Yes, please,' Kelly didn't disguise her eagerness.

Ryan smiled a little at it. 'I'll meet you at the tack-room again, then.'

'Fine,' Kelly agreed with a bright smile in return.

The next day she was at the tack-room ten minutes early. Though Ryan had reminded her of the lesson over lunch, he hadn't needed to. She'd woken up looking forward to it.

Being early, she decided to make herself useful by collecting the bridle and saddle from the shed. The trouble was, there seemed to be an infinite variety of both, and she was still scratching her head over which to pick, when the door opened behind her.

She turned with a smile that slipped a fraction on seeing it wasn't Ryan, but Jeff. 'Oh, hello. I didn't know you were back.'

'I haven't been for long,' the stockman replied. 'I saw you coming in here—wondered if you might need some help,' he added tentatively.

'Well, I do actually. I want to be ready before Ryan comes, but I'm not sure which bridle or saddle to choose.'

'Yeah, I heard he was teaching you to ride. What sort of horse has he given you?'

'He's called Enniscorthy,' Kelly said with slight pride of ownership.

Jeff's brows rose at the name. 'Enniscorthy? 'Struth, Ryan must have been feeling generous.'

'What do you mean?' she quizzed in response.

'Just that he's a pretty fine animal,' he explained.

'Oh.' Kelly was disconcerted. Despite his being kept in the stables, she'd assumed Enniscorthy couldn't be very valuable.

'Not that you don't deserve the best,' Jeff went on hastily, thinking he'd offended her.

Kelly gave a distracted smile as she wondered why Ryan had chosen such a horse for her. Then, finding no answer, she watched the stockman selecting the right tack.

When they emerged from the shed, it was to see Ryan approaching from the yards. He spotted Kelly first and started to smile, but the smile faded when he recognised the man behind her.

'Jeff,' he greeted the other man with a brief nod. 'You're back, then.'

'Half an hour or so,' Jeff confirmed, seemingly oblivious to any undercurrents as he ran on, 'I heard you're teaching Kelly to ride. Thought I'd come and watch for a while . . . if neither of you minds.'

Ryan remained grimly silent, but his disapproval came over in waves, prompting Kelly to put in hastily, 'To be honest, Jeff, I'd prefer you didn't. I feel nervous enough without an audience looking on.'

'Oh, well——' Jeff's shrug didn't quite hide his disappointment. 'Perhaps another time. Good luck for now . . .'

'Thanks,' Kelly called over her shoulder, already following Ryan, who'd picked up the tackle and departed without a word.

When she caught up with him, it was to be slid a look of accusation that had her saying, 'Be fair, Ryan. I discouraged him, didn't I? Short of being downright rude, what more could I do?'

'Yes, OK.' Grudgingly, he accepted her point, before muttering, 'Rudeness probably wouldn't work, anyway. I suspect Jeff has some masochistic tendencies.'

'Oh, thanks!' Kelly snapped back, and, forgetting any desire to improve the atmosphere, she forged ahead of him.

This time *he* had to catch up with her. 'Hey, what did I say?'

'Nothing. It's what you implied,' she sniffed in reply.

'All right,' he tried again, 'what did I imply?'

'Only that he'd have to be a masochist to be interested in me,' she retorted, sure she didn't need to state the obvious.

'I implied that?' Ryan was genuinely surprised at first, then he drawled back, 'Well, there you are. I must be smarter than I'd realised.'

Kelly recognised mockery when she heard it, but found herself unusually stuck for an answer.

And, before she could come up with one, Ryan continued, 'Come on, Kelly, I didn't mean anything like that. In fact, I'd be willing to bet most of the men on the station fancy you... Those not needing glasses, at any rate,' he added with a smile.

For a moment Kelly was silent, not sure how to react to such blatant flattery. It was so plainly an attempt to humour her into a better mood.

'OK, you don't have to overdo it,' she finally replied. 'I forgive you.'

Ryan didn't know how to react to this for a second either, but he eventually chose to laugh at the sheer nerve of the girl.

Then they reached the pen where he'd earlier corralled Enniscorthy, and Ryan watched as her face was transformed by a smile. If he'd given her the bay on an impulse, he didn't regret it—not when she smiled like that.

'Well, let's see what you remember.' He handed her the riding tackle to put on and stood back as, with grim concentration, she did it perfectly. Then he bent to offer her a stirrup up.

This time Kelly managed to mount more gracefully, and sit firmly in the saddle.

'Right, today you're going to learn how to use the reins,' Ryan began, and went on first to emphasise the importance of handling them as lightly as possible, so as not to ruin the horse's mouth.

'But doesn't it hurt him, anyway?' Kelly frowned.

'It shouldn't,' Ryan asserted, 'if you're doing it right. You have to hold the reins a certain way. If you give me your left hand...'

Kelly did so, and hid any sense of shyness as he gently interlaced her fingers with the reins.

'These over the strap, the rest under, and the same with your right hand.'

'It seems a complicated way of holding them.'

'Possibly—and some riders don't bother. But it's the way that'll allow you the most control with the least effort... And we do want to learn properly, don't we?' he enquired with a wry air.

'Of course,' Kelly said in a similar vein. 'As my mother used to say, "if you can't do something well..."'

'Don't do it at all?' Ryan suggested when she paused for thought.

'No, actually, it went—"if you can't do something well, then what the hell",' Kelly faithfully quoted her mother's relaxed philosophy on life, and was surprised at Ryan's laughing with her.

'You thought a lot of her, didn't you?' he asked.

'Yes, I did,' she confirmed, but said no more.

And Ryan, even if he felt her loyalty was misplaced, still admired her for it.

He continued with the lesson, demonstrating how to use the reins to give the horse direction. She seemed to absorb it fairly well, but looked horrified when he told her to also use her feet.

'You want me to kick him?' she said in disbelief.

'Just with your heels.' He added, 'A small kick on the side of his belly—and no, it won't hurt him. So, are you ready to do a few turns of the pen?'

'I suppose.'

'Don't sound so confident.'

'I'm not.' She pulled a doubtful face.

'You'll do fine,' he assured, and stepped back to allow her room.

Gently, Kelly pressed on Enniscorthy's flanks and carefully tugged on the reins. She felt a sense of wonder when he actually moved forwards, and more so when, under Ryan's instruction, she managed to steer him in a new direction.

It still wasn't that easy. She had a fair number of criticisms levelled at her by Ryan, though he seemed to be trying a more polite approach. Today, at any rate, she wasn't accused of slouching, so much as 'leaning forwards slightly'. And if a couple of times she dropped the reins, only to forget the proper way to hold them, he patiently reminded her.

By the end of the lesson, she felt she'd achieved something, and it was she who asked, 'Same time tomorrow?'

'Sure,' he smiled back, then, helping her down, trusted her to take Enniscorthy back to the stables by herself.

Eventually they met every afternoon for a week. She progressed from a sedate walking pace, to a mild trot, to a more exciting canter across the homestead square, until on the last day Ryan allowed her to go for a proper ride. Of course, he accompanied her on his own big grey stallion, and they didn't ride far, just to the nearest well. But, if Kelly knew she was on trial, it didn't stop her from enjoying the outing.

When they returned to the stables, Ryan's verdict was, 'Well, you're not quite ready for the Olympics or even the Katherine Show, but I suppose you'll do.'

If not exactly high praise, Kelly knew him well enough by now to take it as a pass, and respond with a wry, 'Thanks.'

It was only later she felt a sense of anticlimax. For, now the lessons were finished, she assumed she'd see much less of him.

She need not have worried, however, for at lunch the next day Ryan invited her to ride out with him while he checked the level at one of the waterholes. It set a new pattern for the coming weeks, as they spent most afternoons together, either riding to places within range of the homestead, or going further afield in jeep or plane.

Gradually Kelly was drawn into the life of Kilconnell Downs. Through visiting mustering camps with Ryan, she became a familiar figure to the stockmen, who treated her with an odd but not unpleasant mixture of respect and good humour. They obviously believed she'd come home for good—an idea that Kelly herself no longer considered ridiculous. For she began to love the Outback country, wild as it was, and she let the days slip by, with little thought for the world outside.

Once Ryan took her with him in the pick-up to Katherine, thinking she might appreciate being back in 'civilisation'. He left her to shop while he attended to business, but Kelly found there was little she wished to buy, and spent the time strolling around until she was meant to meet Ryan at the jeep.

'Is that all you bought—books?' He indicated the small package she was holding.

'I couldn't think of anything else I wanted,' Kelly said with a shrug.

'No, I suppose Katherine isn't exactly a world centre for fashion,' Ryan grimaced in return.

'Not exactly,' she agreed, before saying, 'I wasn't shopping for clothes, though. I've brought enough with me.'

'Really?' He slanted her a curious glance. 'I always thought women could never have *enough* clothes.'

'Well, now you know differently,' Kelly retorted.

But Ryan still smiled as he admitted, 'I got you something, all the same.'

'You did?' Kelly was more suspicious than grateful as he presented her with a cardboard box.

A grin spread over her face, however, when she opened it to find a wide-brimmed hat, like some of the stockmen wore. Made of suede, it was a cream colour, with a brown leather band around.

'Don't know if it's the right size,' Ryan added, sounding oddly self-conscious.

Kelly tried the hat on, saying, 'It feels right. How does it look?'

'Let's see.' Ryan gazed at the face tilted up at him, framed by black curls under the slightly too large stetson, and all over again he realised how beautiful she was. But he simply said, 'It should keep the sun off, at least.'

'Yes.' Kelly sighed, wondering why she'd expected anything other than a practical comment from him. 'Thanks a lot,' she added as she remembered her manners.

'It's not much,' Ryan shrugged, then dismissed the whole conversation by suggesting they should start home.

But if he saw his present as 'not much', it was precious to Kelly. For she took it as a sign that Ryan had grown to like her a little. And, though she didn't analyse why, that liking had become important to her.

She was never sure of it, however, even as the weeks passed and he continued to take her everywhere. At times she wondered if he didn't seek her company simply to please Paddy. At others, she felt he was watching and waiting for something to happen. She supposed it might just be her departure, though he no longer mentioned the subject.

And it was to Paddy she finally admitted her plans for the future. His cast was to be removed that week and, when he suggested taking her on a trip round the rest of Australia, she felt she had to tell him of her chances of a place at university. By then she'd been on the station for almost two months, and she expected the results of her entrance exam any time.

Naturally, Paddy was surprised and disappointed that he might lose her soon. But he accepted the situation with resignation.

Kelly's attitude wasn't so different. Though Paris and the Sorbonne had begun to seem like a very distant dream, there was still no place for her here. She might be the daughter of the house to the men, but never to Ryan. She'd just to look at his face when anyone referred to her as his sister, to realise he disliked the idea of her being regarded as part of the Devlin family.

How *he* actually regarded her, Kelly didn't dare speculate. His behaviour was so unpredictable, indulgent one moment, short-tempered the next. Like when the letter arrived...

It came only days later, on the morning before Paddy was due to fly to Katherine for the removal of his cast. A stockman had made the regular run to collect mail from the railhead at Larrimah, and brought it up to the house. Unfortunately, Kelly was out at the time and it was intercepted by Meg Donaldson.

Perhaps the Australian woman didn't know its significance, but there was something very deliberate about the way she handed it over at the lunch table.

'This came for you.' She placed it in front of Kelly with a small flourish, then, pausing to make sure she had a full audience, added, 'Just fancy—all the way from Egypt.'

Just fancy! Kelly had grown to loathe the expression, and gave the housekeeper a hard glance before she looked across the table to Ryan. He was already staring at her, a half-scowl etched on his features. He'd obviously guessed who the letter's sender was.

So did Paddy as he smiled, 'That must be from your friend Jay. He's filming in Egypt, isn't he?'

'Yes, he is.' Kelly nodded in confirmation but, despite Paddy's expectant air, she made no move to pick up the letter.

'Well, obviously you can't wait to read it,' Ryan said, his tone sarcastic.

And Paddy reproved gently, 'Now, son, maybe Kelly prefers to read it in private.'

'I'm sure she does,' Ryan agreed, but with thinly veiled contempt.

Clearly, his view of her relationship with Jay hadn't changed, despite the many hours they'd spent together.

It was with a mixture of hurt and anger that Kelly snatched up the letter to rip it open. She already had a good idea of its contents. There was a note from Jay, a cheque folded into two, and an enclosed letter, stamped 'University of Sorbonne'.

She read Jay's note first. It didn't take long. After a brief reference to her latest financial position, he complained of being overworked, over-budget and already overdue in his shooting schedule. And, though he sent his love at the end, no one could possibly view it as other than an affectionate letter from a friend.

She handed it over to Paddy to read and, as he did so, she stared challengingly at Ryan. He must have realised the letter was innocent, for his eyes shifted to the cheque slip she'd yet to unfold.

Kelly had been given a rough estimate of how much to expect from her mother's small percentage, but that had been before *Sunset Gold* had proved a box office hit. She glanced almost uninterestedly at the cheque, then did a doubletake at the amount. Over four hundred thousand American dollars!

Dumbstruck, she handed it to Paddy. She'd told him of her prospects, but the amount came as a surprise to him, too.

'God help us!' he exclaimed, then passed it to Ryan. 'Just look at that, son. Would you believe it?'

Kelly had the satisfaction of watching Ryan's impassive expression become one of astonishment for an instant.

'It's my mother's royalties from her last film,' she said.

And stiffly he replied, 'Congratulations. It seems you didn't need any rich relations, after all.'

She frowned, hearing echoes of another conversation. It was on their journey here—when she'd joked to Jeff about the Devlins being her rich Australian relations. Ryan had been mad then, thinking she was after their money. He was mad now, realising she wasn't. She couldn't win!

Paddy, almost forgotten, looked from one scowling face to another, and decided a distraction was called for. 'Would that be your notification from the University?' he indicated the other enclosed envelope.

'Yes, I think so.' Kelly nodded and quickly dropped her eyes away from Ryan's as she picked it up.

'University?' he echoed, his voice harsh.

And Paddy recognised he'd distracted them from the cheque, only to settle on a subject which might be even more controversial. He saw Kelly flush guiltily as she kept her head down. It was plain she hadn't explained things to Ryan and wasn't going to now.

So he did it for her, forcing lightness into his voice as he said, 'Kelly's been keeping it as a surprise. She's applied to get into the University of Sorbonne to study languages, and she's been waiting to hear if she's passed the entrance exam.'

In response, Ryan almost growled at Kelly, 'Is that true?'

'Yes,' she admitted in a mumble.

'Why didn't you say anything?' he demanded, not bothering to conceal his anger from Paddy now. 'Why the hell didn't you tell me?'

'Why should I?' Kelly returned on the defensive. 'You wouldn't have believed me, anyway. You never do... Or you would have just laughed at the idea that I might be clever enough to get into university.'

Ryan's expression darkened further, but he didn't deny her accusations, asking instead, 'Well, are you?'

Kelly didn't know yet. She'd opened the envelope, then become caught up in arguing with him.

She took out the letter enclosed, and for a moment felt a dread of reading the contents. She assumed it was fear of having failed until she unfolded the typed document. Then her eyes scanned the page and her heart plummeted at the result, and she realised she was quite, quite wrong.

'Well?' Ryan demanded once more.

And Kelly had to swallow the lump in her throat before answering, 'I've got a place, yes.'

There was a moment's silence while the two men digested the news.

Paddy made an effort, saying, 'Sure, isn't that wonderful?'

It was Ryan who didn't hide his feelings. He didn't pretend it was wonderful or anything else. He just gave Kelly a cold, hard stare. Then he stood up, knocking his chair back in the process, and without another word walked from the room.

'Wonderful,' Kelly echoed, trying to laugh when she felt like crying.

And Paddy said, as near to criticism as he ever came, 'You should have told him, lass. You should have told him.'

'I know,' she admitted quietly. 'But he gets so angry at times. I mean, look at the way he just reacted.'

'Oh, Kelly girl, that wasn't anger. Not really,' Paddy sighed in return.

'It looked pretty much like anger to me,' Kelly argued, her face becoming sullen.

'It's only Ryan, his way of . . .'

'. . . Of what?'

Paddy, however, shook his head, thinking better of explaining Ryan's motives.

'Well, I don't understand him.' Kelly masked her own hurt as she pushed away her untouched meal.

Before Paddy could comment, they were interrupted by Meg Donaldson, reappearing to announce that one of the men was waiting to fly him to his hospital appointment in Katherine. With the reassurance that Ryan would calm down, he had to leave Kelly for the afternoon.

To avoid the housekeeper's curious gaze, she went to her room. She still held the letter from the university crumpled in her hand. She smoothed it out, hoping she might have misread the wording. But it still had 'PASS' in block capitals.

Tears gathered in Kelly's eyes as she suddenly recognised the truth. She hadn't wanted that pass. She had wanted a 'FAIL' that would have allowed her the excuse to stay. And now?

If she had any pride, she would leave as soon as possible. For nothing had changed, and nothing ever would. Ryan might pretend to like her for Paddy's sake, but she would always be Rhea Cormack's daughter to him—a girl who slept around.

The thought made Kelly turn her face into a pillow and allow the tears to fall. At least there was no one to see them. No one to wonder why she was crying. No one but herself.

And she didn't have to wonder. She knew. She was crying because she hated Ryan Devlin. Crying because she loved him, too. Hopelessly.

CHAPTER TEN

IT WAS late in the afternoon before Kelly felt sufficiently composed to leave her room. She'd cried until her eyes were red-rimmed, and then she'd faced up to the only course open to her—to get away from Kilconnell Downs.

But first she had to say goodbye to the place in her own way. So she changed into her riding clothes and walked slowly across to the stables. There she saddled up Enniscorthy, sad to realise it would be the last time.

They didn't go far, just to the nearest waterhole. It was enough to imprint on her mind the sights and sounds of the bush, and feel again its sense of timelessness. Wild country, perhaps, yet Kelly had come to see beyond the heat and the dust and the harshness, come to love the challenge it offered and the freedom. She could have made a life here. She knew she could—with the right man.

Only he had never really seen her. Not in that light. At best he'd treated her like a little sister, and at worst like a permissive delinquent who had to be watched so she wouldn't stray.

The trouble was, she'd forgotten the worst when they'd been at their best. He'd taken her everywhere, he'd smiled at her and laughed with her and been kind to her. And, somewhere along the way, she'd fallen in love with him.

Kelly could no longer hide from the fact. When she returned to the homestead, it was to go to the living-room, where the array of photographs stood on the piano. She picked up the most recent one of Ryan, and felt her heart turn over.

She imagined the life they might have shared, and knew then she really wasn't like her mother. She might

love with the same impulsiveness. She might love as un-
wisely. But she would love only once—this time and this
man.

She placed the photograph back on the piano and
tightly shut her eyes. She had to learn to control her
tears, or she would upset Paddy even more over her
sudden departure.

It turned out, however, that she didn't have to worry
about putting on a brave face—that evening, at least.
For some time later Meg Donaldson appeared to relay
messages that neither of the men would be there for
dinner.

Ryan had apparently decided he was needed at one of
the mustering camps and was likely to be away for some
days. At the same time, Paddy had radioed from
Katherine to explain that the Cessna had developed
engine trouble, forcing them to stay overnight in the
town. With both absent, the housekeeper suggested, less
than politely, that Kelly could fend for herself. Kelly
agreed, pleased to be spared the woman's company.

It also gave her more time to plan her departure and
the excuses she might offer Paddy. Though determined
to leave as soon as possible, she now had a few days'
grace while Ryan was away from the homestead.

She spent the evening alone, cooking and eating her
meal in the kitchen. She tried not to think too much of
the future ahead of her, only to end up thinking too
much of Ryan and things that would never be, till once
again tears began to gather in her eyes.

Impatient with herself, she dashed them away and rose
from the table. Needing a distraction, she went to take
a shower before bed. But, just as she was about to step
into the shower, the house was plunged into darkness.
It happened so suddenly, she felt a little frightened for
a second, until she worked out the lights must have fused.
Then she groped for her towelling robe and, slipping it
on, padded barefoot to the kitchen. She had no idea
where the fuse-box was, or even how to repair one, but

she assumed there must be candles kept for such an occasion.

The main problem was finding them without a light to look by in the first place. She banged into a couple of chairs before making it across to the cupboards beside the sink, then she spent ten minutes playing guessing games with various boxes until she discovered matches but no candles. She was just about to give up and go to bed when she heard footsteps on the veranda outside, followed by a voice calling her name.

She groped her way back out of the kitchen, along the corridor to the screen door, where a figure was standing, holding a torch.

'It's me—Jeff,' the stockman identified himself at her approach. 'I thought I'd better come up—see you were all right,' he added when she pushed open the door.

'Fine, apart from the lights. They seem to have fused.'

'No, it's the generator that's packed up. Listen.'

Kelly frowned, hearing nothing, then it struck her that was what Jeff meant. Normally the generator hummed day and night, background noise that one ceased to notice after a while. 'Will it take long to repair?'

Jeff shrugged. 'Difficult to say. You should have some camping lamps in the house.'

Kelly pulled a face. 'The question is where.'

'I'll come in and have a look...if you want me to, I mean,' Jeff offered hesitantly, conscious that she was wearing only a towelling robe.

'Be my guest,' Kelly said as she waved him inside and fell in step behind him.

Despite his torch, it took them some time to find a couple of gas lamps, tucked behind a flour barrel in the larder. One proved easy to light, but the other seemed to be out of commission. Jeff began dismantling it while Kelly made them a cup of coffee on the gas stove.

They were sitting, chatting casually, when once more footsteps resounded on the wooden porch. But this visitor didn't wait at the outer door, as they both heard it swinging on its hinges.

'Who can that be?' Kelly frowned.

'Ryan?' Jeff suggested doubtfully.

Kelly shook her head, dismissing the idea. 'Paddy, maybe.'

Then a voice called her name, with an impatient edge that was terribly familiar.

'Oh, hell,' she muttered to herself, forgetting Jeff for a second.

'What's wrong? It's Ryan,' he said, not realising he was, in fact, answering his own question.

The next moment Ryan himself appeared in the doorway. He stopped short at the sight of Jeff, seated at the table. Then his eyes flicked to Kelly, and she knew almost in that first instant what he was thinking.

Jeff seemed oblivious, smiling and saying, 'Didn't expect you back tonight, mate.'

It drew a clipped, 'Obviously,' from Ryan, still standing by the door, still staring at Kelly.

She stared back, stubbornly silent, head at a defiant angle. She wasn't going to explain herself.

It was Jeff who volunteered, 'Generator's packed up, I'm afraid. So I came up to the house to see if Kelly was all right.'

'She looks all right to me,' Ryan responded, his eyes raking Kelly's appearance before he added, 'Apart from the fact that she isn't dressed, of course. But I don't suppose you objected to that.'

The accusation was plain enough now, but, instead of an immediate denial, Jeff flushed as if he actually had something to be guilty about.

Kelly considered it was time to intervene, snapping at Ryan, 'I was taking a shower when the generator went... *And that's all!*'

'Really?' It was a derisive mutter as he took a couple of steps away from the door, nearer the light. 'Then maybe you'd like to explain why your hair's dry.'

'Why don't you use your imagination?' Kelly suggested with biting scorn. 'After all, it already seems to be working overtime.'

'It has good cause to, in your case,' he ground back, fists clenching at his sides.

The gesture did not go unnoticed by Jeff, though he'd been slow to grasp that it was Kelly, not himself, who was in danger from Ryan's temper.

'Oh, come on, mate, she's not going to look at an ordinary bloke like me,' he appealed almost amiably. 'And besides, you can't believe I'd try it on with your sister.'

'Can't I?' Ryan echoed, not in the least bit amiably. 'So tell me—why have you been sniffing round her ever since she got here?'

The question brought another flush to the stockman's face, this time as much anger as embarrassment. 'OK, maybe I have,' he admitted, getting to his feet. 'But I'm not the only one, am I?'

A dreadful silence followed, a silence in which Jeff already began to regret his rash words, while Kelly shut her eyes, wishing herself elsewhere.

Then Ryan challenged, 'Meaning?'

'Look, this is ridiculous,' Kelly said in a desperate bid to distract them.

But Ryan ignored her, repeating on a threatening note, *'Meaning?'*

'All right, though you'll probably fire me for it,' Jeff muttered back, 'you might as well know. Everyone's noticed it—the way you treat Kelly like she's your property, the way you watch her all the time. The men think it's pretty funny.'

At this, Ryan's face went rigid, explosion imminent, and once more Kelly tried to rescue the situation, saying, 'It's not that funny, really. It's just that Ryan doesn't trust me very much.'

But Ryan wouldn't play along. 'That's not what he's suggesting... *Is it,* Jeff?'

Jeff looked trapped, sorry he'd ever started this. When Ryan continued to stare at him, demanding an answer, he reluctantly admitted, 'No, it isn't.'

'Well, you're right about one thing, Jeff,' Ryan returned with a short harsh laugh. 'As from now, you can consider yourself fired.'

For a moment Jeff was plainly stunned. Though he'd put the idea in the other man's head, he'd counted on their friendship for it not to be taken up.

'You can't be serious!' came from Kelly, jumping to her feet to confront Ryan.

'Can't I?' Cold grey eyes said he was deadly serious.

'It's unfair and you know it!' she flared back.

'Don't bother, Kelly.' Jeff placed a restraining hand on her arm, not wanting to cause any more trouble for her. 'As far as I'm concerned, he can take his job and shove it,' he added with a bitter glance at Ryan, before picking up his torch and striding from the room.

Kelly delayed just long enough to throw at Ryan, 'Happy now?' then went after the stockman, guided by the receding torchlight ahead. She managed to catch him up on the porch steps, apologising breathlessly, 'Oh, God, Jeff, I'm sorry. I don't know why he has to behave like that.'

'It's all right, it's not your fault,' Jeff reassured, pressing the hand she'd laid on his arm. 'I should find another job pretty easy.'

'But you can't want to leave—you've worked here for years,' she protested.

'Almost ten,' he recalled with a sigh, then shrugged philosophically. 'Not much I can do about it now, though. Teach me to keep my big mouth shut.'

'It wasn't you.' Kelly knew full well who was the real target of Ryan's anger. 'I'll speak to Paddy when he returns. Maybe he'll make Ryan give you your job back.'

Jeff shook his head. 'There'd be no point, Kelly, even if he did. You see, it's Ryan I have to work with. And I don't think he's going to forgive me.'

'I don't see what *he* has to forgive. After all, he started it—jumping to conclusions.'

'Perhaps, but I didn't help, saying what I did about you and him.'

'Well, yes, you were way off-base there,' Kelly stated positively.

'If you're sure...' Jeff still had his doubts, but he felt there was little he could do. He noticed her shivering and said with reluctance, 'You'd better go inside.'

Chilled in her towelling robe, Kelly nodded and, after another fervent apology for the night's events, went back into the bungalow.

Not up to a second fight with Ryan, she decided it would be wisest to go straight to bed. Without a light, she felt her way down the hall and along the back corridor. She did it quietly, tensing for any sound of footsteps behind her, before breathing a sigh of relief when she reached her bedroom door.

Her relief was short-lived, however, as she slipped inside. She noticed first the lit gas lamp resting on her bedside table, then the figure seated in the basket chair in the far corner. She almost took fright and backed out of the room, but recovered sufficient nerve to demand, 'What do you want?'

Ryan took time in responding, his voice low and disembodied as it came from the shadows, 'What do you imagine I want?'

Kelly shook her head, in no mood for guessing games. Then a thought struck her. 'Knowing you, it's to check I came back alone. *Right?*'

'Partly,' he admitted, without any attempt to justify the action.

'Well, I have—so perhaps you'd like to go now,' she said through gritted teeth.

It was plainly more an order than a request, but he made no move to obey. He just sat there, hidden in shadow, a pair of hostile eyes watching her.

Yet Kelly still felt anger rather than fear. She'd spent the day crying her heart out over this man. And now here he was—treating her like dirt again, making her seem a fool for loving him at all.

Sarcastically, she ran on, 'Unless, of course, you'd like to look under my bed. Or maybe in the wardrobe? Let's see, shall we?'

She stamped across the room to throw open the wardrobe door.

Out of his chair before she'd finished, Ryan came up beside her to slam the door shut. Then, grabbing her before she could move away, he rapped out, 'It isn't funny, damn you!'

'Who's laughing?' she retorted, wincing as his fingers bit into her arm.

'*You are!*' he accused. 'Laughing inside because you know *exactly* how I feel.'

'Well, what do you expect me to do?' she shot back. 'Hang my head while you moralise at me, sit in judgement over me, when all the time——'

'All right, you don't have to say it!' Ryan cut in harshly. 'I admit the fact. The whole world seems to know it, anyway.'

The whole world, however, didn't include Kelly, who suddenly hadn't a clue what they were talking about.

'And maybe you're right. Maybe it is a joke,' he pursued, lips twisting in a humourless smile.

'What is?' Kelly was now totally bewildered.

Ryan scowled at her, not believing she needed to ask, growling in angry frustration, 'That nothing you do seems to matter. That I still go on wanting you—wanting you just like everybody else.'

'W-wanting me?' Kelly repeated the words as though they made no sense to her. And they didn't. Not really. If he'd kissed her a few times, it had always been as a way of humiliating her. So how could he possibly want her? It was a joke, as he said. A cruel, awful joke.

'Don't you know?' Ryan registered her disbelief with an incredulity of his own.

Slowly Kelly shook her head.

'You must know!' Ryan insisted, hurting her as his grip tightened again. 'I've wanted you from the first moment I set eyes on you, the very first. And I've never stopped wanting you. I want you now,' he admitted on a harsh note of desire.

It scared Kelly. The whole thing scared her. Not a joke. Not a game. Just a situation she wasn't ready for at all.

'Don't——' She turned her head away as he bent to kiss her.

Hoarsely he demanded, 'Why not me, Kelly? Why not?'

'Please——' She heard the break in her own voice, the weakness, and tried to push him away.

But he kept hold of her, his eyes searching her face. 'Do I have to beg? Is that it?'

Kelly shook her head, pained at his lack of understanding. She didn't want him to beg. She just wanted him to say he loved her.

Instead he urged, 'Then let me, Kelly...let me,' in a low, persuasive murmur as his eyes held hers.

It was desire, not love, that Kelly saw in those eyes, heard in his voice. Desire—an unlasting emotion, spent and gone soon.

Yet she was caught as she stared back at him—love, not desire, in her eyes. Love she imagined he'd recognise without words. So she made words unnecessary, placing her hands on his shoulders, reaching up to touch the side of his face with her lips.

The lightest of kisses, a shy rather than bold gesture, it confused Ryan even more. Oddly sweet, and not fitting his image of her as experienced. And for a split second he wondered if all the time he'd been wrong.

But it was an unacceptable thought when he, like Kelly, wanted this moment—untroubled by conscience, grabbed before it could be lost. A thought that he rejected as he began kissing her in return. Gently at first, his hands coming up to frame her face, then with increasing hunger as control slipped away.

Kelly reacted instinctively, parting her lips for him, offering him the intimacy he demanded, trembling at the force of it. For now she was sure of her fierce, whole-hearted love for this man, if still a little afraid.

A little shy, too. She dropped her eyes away when he finally stepped back to look at her, nervously stepping back herself when his hand reached out to untie the belt of her robe, lifting her eyes again to catch the sudden uncertainty in his.

'You're not stopping me now. You *can't*!' he said with the harshness of disbelief.

Not surprisingly, she backed away again.

But he made no move towards her, simply repeating, 'You can't, Kelly.'

Only this time it was on an almost anguished note—appeal, not demand—so that Kelly understood the choice was hers. He wasn't going to force her. It had been unfair to even consider he would.

He just stood there, waiting for an answer, and when none came he muttered, with a bitter laugh that mocked himself, 'God, I'm a fool! I should have realised. And perhaps I asked for it. But it's a dangerous game, Kelly. I'd be careful of the men you choose to play it with.'

At last Kelly found her voice, choking out, 'It isn't a game.'

'Isn't it?' Ryan echoed flatly, as if he no longer cared, and began to turn away.

He was halted by Kelly crying impulsively, 'I'll show you!' her hands already fumbling at her robe, untying the belt, letting the garment drop in an untidy heap on the floor. Each action was done in jerky, uncoordinated haste, a task to be got over as quickly as possible.

Ryan stared, stunned at first, then compelled, fasci-nated, his desire renewed at the sight of her, small, slender and perfect. Her skin was a deep, dusky colour in the shadowy light, her breasts more beautiful than he remembered. The whole of her was more beautiful, he decided as his gaze travelled down her body, lingering, touching, already making love to her in his mind.

Only one thing spoilt his pleasure. The fact it wasn't shared. That was plain from the way she hung her head, her face hidden as if ashamed.

Again the thought came. Was he wrong? And again he shut it out. He couldn't be wrong!

Kelly's thoughts were in turmoil, too. She could sense him watching her, could almost feel his eyes running over her skin. But the longer he just stood there, the more her courage deserted her, until finally she became convinced he must have changed his mind.

'I-It's all right . . . if you don't w-want . . . it's OK,' she stammered out, at the same time scooping up the robe to shield her body.

'Don't want you?' came in a stunned echo from Ryan, wanting her more than ever and proving it as he closed the gap between them to take the robe from her hands and draw her to him. His arms enclosed her shivering frame, pressing her to the warmth and strength of his, in a tender embrace that seemed more loving than sexual.

So tender, Kelly could almost pretend it was love he was offering as she buried her face in his chest, and felt his body shudder against the softness of her own.

Then a hand came under her hair, tilting her head back, and once more his mouth fastened on hers, in a kiss of growing urgency and need. Eventually he led her towards the bed, still kissing her as he gently laid her back against the covers.

When he left her, it was to discard his own clothing. He did so carelessly, his eyes fixed on her nakedness. They told Kelly how beautiful he found her, before shading with soft mockery when she finally hid from their wandering, searching gaze.

With the quilt pulled up to her neck, Kelly supposed her shyness must seem absurd to him. She tried to act blasé, watching as he shrugged off his shirt to reveal a strongly muscled chest, coarsened with dark blond hair that tapered down to his waist. But if she caught her breath, seeing beauty in the sheer powerful masculinity of his body, her act was ruined by the quick aversion of her eyes when he began stripping off his jeans.

Perhaps he noticed, for he asked quietly, 'Shall I turn off the lamp?'

She nodded, still not looking at him, and felt her heart trip over as the room was suddenly pitched into darkness. A different sort of fear gripped her now. The fear of disappointing. For what did she know about love-making?

Nothing, unless she counted silly, adolescent conversations at the finishing school, where some girls boasted of their exploits. The mechanics of sex, not the art of loving. And with experience of neither, how she could hope to please him?

By the time he climbed into bed beside her, she couldn't even move. Terrified of doing the wrong thing, she just lay there, rigid with tension, staring into darkness. She almost flinched when his arms reached out for her, and almost confessed her ignorance—her innocence—at the first shock of his bare skin against hers. Only it was far too late for such a confession—far too late to stop him, even if she wanted to.

And she didn't. Not when desire was already drowning out fear as his hands pressed her gently back against the pillows and his mouth claimed hers once more, kissing her until she was breathless, before moving to softly bite the nape of her neck, to trail over her skin in a slow path downwards.

When his mouth covered the peak of her breast, Kelly gasped at the strange, unnerving sensation of it, too startled initially to recognise the spasm that shuddered through her body wasn't pain. But as his lips continued to pull gently, then suck hungrily, there was no doubting her response. She was unable to stifle her small pleasure noises, and after a while she didn't even try, exciting him in turn with her sweet moans of desire. Inhibition was completely forgotten as she held his head to her breast, then wantonly offered the other for the caress of his tongue, the sensual bite and play of his mouth. Her fears were forgotten as she realised he, too, was drawing pleasure, his breathing becoming more ragged, while perspiration dampened his skin.

When he eventually lifted his mouth away, it was to capture hers again, at the same time pushing back the covers to spread a hand against the flat of her stomach. A hand that slowly slid downwards, following the curve of her hips, angling into the soft skin of her thighs, infinitely slowly, until he roused a tormenting ache that actually wanted his hand to touch the intimate place it sought—warm and moist, ready for him, made more so as the gentle stroke of knowing fingers drew a startled sob from her throat.

She arched against him, breaking any last vestige of restraint in Ryan. Confident that she now wanted him with the same urgency, he poised above her and lifting her body to his, took in one thrust what was so willingly, lovingly, being offered.

Beyond thought or fear, the first tearing pain came as a bitter shock to Kelly. She cried out with it, then went absolutely rigid, nails digging reflexively in his back.

Ryan understood instantly, groaning in anguish, 'Oh, no! God, no!' as he let her punish him for what he had done.

But, when he tried to draw away, Kelly clutched at his shoulders. She could not let it end like this. She wanted him to love her completely—love her in the only way he knew how.

'Please…it's all right,' she said, her voice a soft, husky murmur in the darkness.

Wanting her as much as ever, Ryan made some sound, a throaty acceptance of the gift offered him, and took it gently, unselfishly, soothing away the hurt he'd caused in a sweet, drugging kiss, before controlling the fierce urge of his desire to make slow, gentle love to her.

Gradually that very gentleness became a fine torment for Kelly, creating such a longing that she instinctively lifted her body to his. Reaching for him, opening to him, moving with him, she invited the harder, more demanding thrust of his flesh against hers. And, if she cried out once more, this time it was at the pleasure he gave her, in a tide so strong she could only cling to him, drown with him, in that small death of ecstasy as fulfillment came and he called out her name.

Afterwards they lay together, limbs still entwined, holding each other close. Too dazed to talk, Kelly was unable to believe any experience could be so beautiful, while a more worldly Ryan knew it had been something rare and perfect.

Even when their breathing quietened and a sense of reality returned, Kelly had no desire to talk. For there was nothing to say. Only that she loved him. And she would not trap him with those words.

He sounded guilty enough when he eventually spoke, with a low, hoarse appeal of, 'How could I have been so wrong...so blind?'

'It doesn't matter any more,' Kelly murmured back, a simple statement of truth.

And, whatever he made of it, Ryan echoed softly, 'Not now, no,' as he cradled her body to his.

But he remained awake far into the night, long after Kelly fell asleep, her head pillowed on his shoulder, warm in his arms, with no need to imagine the hand gently stroking her hair.

CHAPTER ELEVEN

'RYAN, where are you? Ryan?' a voice was calling, and at first Kelly thought it was part of her dream.

Then she opened her eyes and heard the voice again, accompanied by a firm knock on the room next door. She'd barely time to realise it was Meg Donaldson, when footsteps started approaching her own bedroom.

'No, don't!' she cried out, but already too late, as the housekeeper, with a peremptory knock, stuck her head round the door.

Noticing Kelly was awake, she launched into asking, 'Is it true? Has Ryan re——' before her eyes switched to the shape, sleeping face-down, on the far side of the bed.

It was impossible to rescue the situation, and Kelly didn't even try. She sat up, clutching a sheet to shield herself, and waited for the outburst that was bound to follow.

She didn't have to wait long, as Meg Donaldson hissed at her, 'No wonder you wanted to be alone yesterday! Well, don't think I won't tell Paddy and Ryan. Not that Ryan will be sur——'

Again the Australian woman broke off, this time as the figure lying beside Kelly stirred and began to turn, making her realise that there was no need to tell Ryan of her discovery.

Kelly watched as the housekeeper's face paled with shock, then she glanced at Ryan, hoping he knew the right thing to say.

He'd gone from deep sleep to full wakefulness in a matter of seconds. Yet his only action was to lean back against the headboard. He made no attempt to explain away the situation.

Still, it seemed that Meg did not hold him responsible, for she screeched at Kelly, 'You little whore! You dirty little——'

'That's enough, Meg!' Ryan rapped out before the insult could be repeated.

'Oh no, not nearly enough,' the housekeeper continued on the same hysterical note. 'When I'm finished, every man on the station is going to know that tramp will sleep with anyone. Not that it wouldn't suit her, having them all queuing up to…to…' She finally faltered, mid-sentence.

Not that she'd run out of steam—just nerve. For Ryan had suddenly risen from the bed, stark naked, to drag on his jeans. Dumbstruck, the Australian woman stared at him for a moment, then took fright and fled.

Grabbing up his shirt, Ryan muttered a hasty, 'Don't worry, I'll sort it out,' before striding after her.

Kelly was left there, still clutching her sheet, too numb to move. Throughout the scene, she hadn't uttered a single word. It had seemed too unreal, like a nightmare over which she had no control. So different from the way she'd woken earlier that morning.

Then it had been at the gentle searching of Ryan's hands as the first light of dawn filtered into the room. She'd turned to him, reached for him, and once more they'd made love, only this time with their eyes as well as their bodies. And afterwards, when he'd held her so close that it seemed he never wished to let her go, she'd fallen asleep, a small flame of hope kindling inside her.

Now, as she dressed and waited for him to return, the flame flickered and gradually died. For one hour stretched to two, and then three, until she could no longer pretend that he was simply explaining things to Meg Donaldson. She could no longer convince herself that *she* was the woman important to him.

And, without hope, all she had left was pride. It governed her actions as she began packing and hardened her heart when he finally reappeared.

Ryan gazed in disbelief from the suitcase lying on the bed, to Kelly as she spared him the briefest of glances before continuing to fold her clothes.

Then he crossed to stand at her side, demanding, 'What are you doing?'

'What does it look like I'm doing?' She shrugged, careless and uncaring.

The next second he grabbed her arm and spun her round to face him. 'You're not leaving! You can't! Not now!'

'Personally, I'd say now was a very good time,' she replied, trying to pull free.

'If you mean Meg, I've fixed that,' he dismissed shortly.

'Really? I wonder how.' Her mouth curved in derision.

'If you must know,' he ground back, 'I gave her three months' money, with the promise of another three, on condition she keeps quiet. Then I drove her to meet the train at Larrimah.'

Totally disconcerted, a mumbled, 'Oh,' was all Kelly could come up with.

'Why?' he asked. 'What did you imagine I was doing?'

'Nothing. I didn't even think about it,' she lied outrageously, then quickly distracted him by asking, 'What if she comes back for more money after six months?'

'By that time, it shouldn't matter. The main problem is to make sure everyone understands we are no blood relations to each other. Maybe Jeff'll take care of that for us.'

'Jeff?' Kelly echoed. 'But you sacked him last night!'

'Yes, well ... I *un*sacked him this morning,' Ryan admitted stiffly.

'Oh,' Kelly said again, wondering if he had any more surprises to spring on her.

He did, adding almost as an afterthought, 'Anyway, Meg's gossip won't do us much harm when we're married.'

'*Married?*'

'Yes, of course. The sooner, the better, I think.'

Kelly stared at him in astonishment. Had he really just asked her to marry him? He sounded so cool and dispassionate, as if they were discussing travel arrangements!

'Why?' she finally said.

'Why?' He gave her an exasperated look.

But when Kelly repeated, 'Yes, why?' he seemed to have difficulty finding the answer himself.

He scowled in irritation, started to speak, changed his mind and, after another lengthy pause, eventually came out with, 'Well, for one thing, you might be pregnant.'

'So?' she challenged.

' *"So?"* So we should get married!'

To Kelly, it was the worst of reasons. 'I don't see why. After all, it's almost a family tradition—illegitimacy,' she pointed out, flippancy hiding hurt.

'Maybe, but I'm not going to let any child of mine think it's unwanted,' Ryan countered, so bitterly that Kelly was reminded of his own background and the mother who'd never really wanted him.

In a softer tone she said, 'You don't have to worry. If there's a child, I'll love it.'

'That's not good enough,' he dismissed, voice still harsh. 'We're getting married, whether you wish to or not!'

'Well, I don't!' Kelly ended up snapping, and shrugged off his hand to continue with her packing.

But Ryan proved he had a temper to match as he swept her bag off the bed. It fell face-down, clothes spilling on to the floor, then he dragged her round again. 'So what the hell was last night about? And don't tell me you didn't enjoy it!'

'What if I did?' Kelly's face flamed with a mixture of fury and embarrassment. 'That doesn't mean I have to marry you, does it?'

'You were a virgin, for God's sake!' He made it sound an accusation, much as he had once made her supposed promiscuity. 'You must feel something for me. You have to. Otherwise, why let me be the first?' he demanded.

Evasively Kelly muttered back, 'Somebody had to be.'

It snapped what little control Ryan had left as his hands bit cruelly into her arms. 'Well, I'm going to be the last... *Do you hear me?*'

He shouted so loudly, it would have been difficult *not* to, as Kelly pointed out. 'I imagine the whole station can bloody well hear you.'

Then a dry voice inserted, 'I have to agree,' and it definitely didn't come from Ryan, on the verge of another explosion.

Too involved in their argument, neither had noticed Paddy standing, his foot now unplastered, in the doorway. When they did, Ryan dropped his hands away from Kelly, and they both swivelled round to confront the older man, wondering how much he'd overheard.

Apparently very little, for he sighed, 'What are you two quarrelling about this time?'

'Nothing,' Kelly shrugged, trusting Ryan would follow her lead.

He did anything but, stating bluntly, 'I was just asking her to marry me.'

Appalled, Kelly looked from him to Paddy, expecting to see horror in his eyes. For didn't he regard them as almost brother and sister?

Yet he didn't even seem surprised, and he didn't sound it either, as he enquired wryly, 'From the shouting, would I be right in thinking you've refused him?'

'Yes,' she stated very definitely.

Only to have Ryan qualify, 'For the moment, she has.'

Paddy noticed the quick flash of temper it brought to his daughter's eyes and, shaking his head, advised gently, 'Well, if I were you, son, I'd try a different approach.'

Then, deciding he could do no more, he withdrew from the room as unobtrusively as he'd entered.

Kelly gazed at the empty doorway, totally disconcerted by her father's behaviour. Far from being horrified, he seemed to have just given them his blessing.

It didn't prevent her from rounding on Ryan. 'You shouldn't have said anything.'

'Why not? He knew, anyway.'

'Knew what?'

Ryan hesitated, before replying shortly, 'That I intended asking you.'

'Asking me what?' Kelly was still at a loss.

'To marry me, of course.'

'Oh.' She nodded in understanding, before realising she didn't actually understand at all. 'How *could* he know?'

This time he was very slow in replying, 'Because I told him.'

'You *told* him?' she cried in disbelief. 'You mean, you talked to him this morning?'

'Not this morning, no,' he said, after another lengthy pause.

'Then when?' she demanded.

And Ryan at last reluctantly admitted, 'Yesterday afternoon...in Katherine.'

The admission, however, left Kelly more confused than ever. He had told Paddy *yesterday* that he intended proposing to her? It made no sense.

'How could you have? You went to one of the mustering camps.' She relayed what Meg Donaldson had told her.

'I started out, but I realised I couldn't risk your leaving while I got over being mad with you,' he explained with a wry twist. 'So I drove up to waylay Paddy at the hospital and tell him outright that I wasn't able to treat you like a sister any longer. Well, Paddy's no fool. He understood what I meant. In fact, I think he'd already guessed how I felt about you.'

'That you *wanted* me?' Kelly recalled the words he'd used last night.

But Ryan shook his head. 'More than that, Kelly.'

'More?' Kelly echoed, too frightened to trust what his eyes were suddenly, so clearly, telling her.

'Much more,' he added softly, as he closed the gap between them.

He reached for her and she went, unresisting, into his arms. He did not kiss her, but simply held her to him while he pleaded, 'I can't let you go, Kelly. I just can't. I know it's asking a lot—for you to give up university and Paris. And I know it must seem hard, this life. But if love counts for anything, I'll make you happy,' he promised in a low, unsteady voice.

It was a promise that came true the moment it was given. For finally Kelly recognised the fierce, possessive love he felt for her, and her heart turned over with happiness.

She raised her eyes to his, to confess her own strong, certain love for him, but, caught between wonder and joy, all she could do was smile.

Ryan didn't appear to notice as he went on, 'You might not think it now. I realise I've treated you badly. I was stupid and blind and jealous... But you have to marry me, don't you see?'

'Oh, yes,' Kelly agreed without the slightest hesitation.

Only this was not what Ryan was expecting at all!

'Yes?' he echoed with a near scowl.

'Yes,' Kelly smiled back, 'I'll marry you.'

Yet Ryan still couldn't believe she was making it so easy for him. 'Just like that?'

And when Kelly tacked on, 'Well, on one condition,' he seemed almost relieved.

'All right—accepted,' he said immediately.

'But you haven't heard what it is,' Kelly protested.

'I don't need to. I know I'll end up doing it. Always assuming it's possible, of course,' Ryan grimaced in return.

'I'd say so,' Kelly assured. 'I mean, I just want you to teach me to fly. That's not difficult, is it?' she added with a look of innocence.

Ryan wasn't deceived. He knew perfectly well she was testing her power over him.

'As long as the lessons begin *after* we're married,' he bargained.

'Fine,' she agreed. 'But why after?'

It was Ryan's turn to smile as he said, 'Well, that way, I at least have a few weeks to enjoy married life.'

'Funny.' Kelly threw him a cross look. 'You still don't believe me about that mountain goat, do you?'

This time, Ryan decided it was wiser not to answer, and instead took her hand.

'Where are we going?' Kelly asked, finding herself being pulled after him, along the corridor.

'To tell Paddy before you change your mind,' he informed her without stopping.

'I won't,' Kelly stated, then felt she should slip in, 'I mean, I do *love* you, you know.'

It brought Ryan to a dead halt. 'You love me?'

'Yes, of course.' Kelly smiled a little wickedly. 'What do you think last night was about?'

And, though Ryan remembered asking the very same question and receiving a very different answer, he let it pass, as he hauled her back in his arms to kiss away the smile which had tormented him from the day he'd first met this girl.

But afterwards he growled at her, 'Some day I really might end up strangling you, Kelly Cormack.'

Kelly simply grinned again, confident of his love now, confident enough to ask, 'Will *that* be before or after you marry me?'

Ryan made no response, other than to tighten his grip on her hand, and this time Kelly had to half run to keep up with him as he dragged her the rest of the way to the veranda.

There Paddy was waiting, seated on his favourite chair. He looked from one flushed face to the other and didn't really need to ask, 'Well?'

'Well, I tried a different approach,' Ryan began, smiling.

'And it worked,' Kelly added, laughing.

Paddy's delight was plain as he rose to his feet and, not knowing who to hug first, managed to hug them both at the same time. Then he said in his rich Irish brogue, 'Thank God for that—now maybe I'll be getting a bit of peace round the place!'

A wry comment, it made Kelly smile, before glancing at Ryan as she replied, 'Oh, I wouldn't be too sure about that.'

His mouth forming an amused curve, Ryan drily agreed, 'No, neither would I.'

But Paddy still beamed, certain of one thing at least—of his children's love for each other.

No longer hidden, it was in every look they exchanged, in the way their eyes caught and held, needing no words to express what they felt. A love so strong, Paddy knew it would survive this Outback life.

And, as Ryan placed a warm, protective arm round her, Kelly knew it, too. For she'd found what her poor dead mother never had.

A special kind of love, a love to last a lifetime and beyond.

Harlequin Temptation dares to be different!

Once in a while, we Temptation editors spot a romance that's truly innovative. To make sure *you* don't miss any one of these outstanding selections, we'll mark them for you.

EDITOR'S CHOICE

When the "Editors' Choice" fold-back appears on a Temptation cover, you'll know we've found that extra-special page-turner!

THE

Temptation

EDITORS

Harlequin American Romance

**Romances that go one step farther...
American Romance**

Realistic stories involving people you can relate to and care about.

Compelling relationships between the mature men and women of today's world.

Romances that capture the core of genuine emotions between a man and a woman.

Join us each month for four new titles wherever paperback books are sold.
Enter the world of American Romance.

Coming Next Month

1143   DEVIL AND THE DEEP SEA Sara Craven
Roche Delacroix needs a wife to retain custody of his child. Samma needs an escape from an impossible situation. Their marriage seemed a solution. Yet Samma soon realizes her new life presents just as many problems—the chief one, her stranger husband.

1144   STRANGER AT WINTERFLOODS Mary Lyons
Polly enjoys her quiet life-style on her own farm. Then an attractive stranger descends on her and makes her aware of all she's lacking. But she can't imagine the differences in their worlds—until she steps into his....

1145   JOURNEY OF DISCOVERY Jessica Marchant
No way, Annabel decides, is Caird Gloster going to walk calmly back into her life. Not after her ten years of struggling to raise their daughter alone—a daughter she's never told him about.

1146   CAUGHT IN A DREAM Susanne McCarthy
Cassy is at her wits' end trying to keep her beloved grandfather from being evicted because of his gambling debts. Two wealthy men show an interest in helping her—but the choice between them is far from easy to make!

1147   A NEW DESIRE Leigh Michaels
Exhausted, jet-lagged Whitney Lattimer isn't too pleased when Max Townsend barges into her hotel bedroom telling her what to do. True, he's investigating the trouble at her Kansas City department store, but ordering her around is going too far.

1148   A PROMISE KEPT Annabel Murray
Accompanying her boss to a friend's in Portugal, Pippa is astounded to find the friend is Carlos de Alvarez. Once, years ago, he'd come to see her father and met Pippa in a humiliating situation. She soon discovers that Carlos has not forgotten.

1149   TOO LONG A SACRIFICE Yvonne Whittal
For his own sake, Julia rejected Nathan Corbett, the man she loved. Her pain seemed never ending, and she's just beginning to get over it when he moves into the little village she'd escaped to. And he has Julia's replacement by his side....

1150   BELOVED INTRUDER Patricia Wilson
Beth Craig is young, spirited and free. She has no intention of letting any guardian take over her life—even if he's rich, French and younger than expected. Though it would be nice, once in a while, to be cared for....

Available in February wherever paperback books are sold, or through Harlequin Reader Service:

In the U.S.
901 Fuhrmann Blvd.
P.O. Box 1397
Buffalo, N.Y. 14240-1397

In Canada
P.O. Box 603
Fort Erie, Ontario
L2A 5X3

Keepsake